Keweenaw Grace

Brian K. Holmes

Copyright © 2024 by Brian K. Holmes.

This is a work of fiction. All of the characters, names, incidents, organizations, and dialogue in this novel are either the products of the author's imagination or are used fictitiously.

Printed in the United States of America.

ISBN   Paperback   979-8-21854-561-1

For Judy

Children go where I send thee how will I send thee
I'm gonna send thee one by one,
one for the little bitty Baby
Who was born, born, born in Bethlehem

(Folk Carol)

He will give you peace; take you by the hand
Fill your life with wonder; help you understand
That His love's forever offered up to you
You only need surrender that's all you have to do.

Brian K. Holmes

The Upper and Lower Peninsulas of Michigan

Keweenaw Peninsula

PROLOGUE

Downtown Hancock is a microcosm of the whole Keweenaw Peninsula in the western end of Michigan's Upper Peninsula. From its southern neighbor, the city of Houghton, to the northern tip of the Peninsula at Copper Harbor, lie a string of cities and towns built one hundred and fifty years ago to facilitate the extraction and processing of copper ore. The groups of immigrants from all over Europe landed in New York City and struck out to stake claims and seek their fortunes in northern Michigan, and it was there for the taking. Towns sprung up around successful mine claims and by the 1880's the peninsula, with Calumet in the middle, was one of the richest areas in the entire country. By the beginning of the twentieth century, street cars and electric lights were installed in many of the small towns and prosperity was there for those willing to roll up their sleeves and go down into the mines.

And then it died. Like all booms it tapered off and then for many reasons it became unprofitable to mine copper in the Keweenaw. Many fingers were pointed and accusations were made. The companies blamed the unions; the unions blamed the greedy managers, and in the end the industry simply moved elsewhere for cheaper labor and less regulations. The music stopped right in the middle of the dance.

To the rest of the world it was only a blip, but to the local miners and their families it was like a death in the community. Projects were stopped; bills weren't paid; dreams were put on hold or abandoned, and this fifty mile long strip of land went into hard times for a hundred years. Occasionally businesses started to fulfill local needs, or a dream or a vision would be spawned by an enterprising individual, but for the most part life just slowed down. The two world wars offered opportunities to leave and start anew, so many packed up went south leaving the descendents to hold on waiting for the next big something.

CHAPTER 1

The white smoke rose from the icy waters of Portage Lake, as the frost began its morning recessional from the slate roof tops of the century old buildings on Quincy Street, in the City of Hancock. It was mid October in the northern upper peninsula of Michigan, and the bright sun rose high in the eastern sky. With one cold hand in his jeans pocket, and the other clutching a credit card, Johnny Hendricks vigorously scraped the ice from the wind shield of his old Dodge van. Freezing temperatures had come early to the Keweenaw Peninsula, and the contrasts of the pines, and maples created a colorful mural that only God could take credit for.

Zipping the insulated hooded sweatshirt up close to his chin, he stomped his feet for warmth, and slid his skinny butt across the vinyl seat cover. He was still whipped from the eleven hour drive from Grand Rapids to Hancock the day before, but he was grateful it was over, and ready for a fresh start. Pulling out of the Hancock Motel parking lot under the approach of the blue Hancock Lift Bridge, he slowly eased into the morning city traffic toward downtown, looking for the first restaurant he could find.

As the small flecks of ice dribbled down the windshield to meet the wrath of the wiper blades, he glanced into the rearview mirror at the bloodshot eyes of a blond, curly headed, baby face, stuck on the shoulders of a six foot, 140 pound scrawny frame. This certainly didn't inspire much confidence that he was the world beater that his folks had placed their hopes and money on when they sent him to this outpost so far from the home front in southwest Michigan. At age twenty five, and with all the education he hoped he'd ever need behind him, he was ready to escape the past and explore some different horizons. Ahead on the left, a large sign announced the Kaleva Bakery and Coffee Shop, and with the bonus of a parking spot right in front of the door, he wheeled right up to the curb.

As he pushed through the front door, the heat and aroma of the baking ovens hit him squarely in the face. And with the tenacity inherited from his mother's side of the family, he squeezed his way through the tables to the five-stool counter.

"Coffee?" asked the tired looking waitress as if there were no other option. It was obvious that after three hours of breakfast traffic, she didn't have much left for small talk.

"Please," he responded reaching for the small plastic covered menu. After ordering the pancake special, he spun around on the stool checking out the rest of the coffee shop. He was glad he wore his best wool shirt, Levi jeans and work boots, to help blend in with the working class locals.

"Excuse me," said his counter mate, "can you pass the sugar?"

Johnny slid the sweetener to his left. "Maybe you can help me," he said. "I'm looking for an empty building to rent here in Hancock."

The waitress came over with Johnny's coffee, a spoon, and the advice.

"Check the bulletin board over by the front door," she nodded. "The locals place their want ads on it 'cause it's free."

Johnny took a sip of coffee, and made his way through the patrons lined up waiting for a table.

Bulletin boards are universal; want ads, business cards, pictures of lost animals, and people wanting to trade their specialty for money. Up in the right hand corner, next to a local dog groomer was an ad for a local store front. For sale or lease, call H. Aho, with the phone number and address. He copied the information and made his way back to a stack of hot pancakes and sausages thinking that at the moment, his stomach held priority over his immediate future. The waitress knew Mrs. Aho, said she was a regular, and gave him directions to her home. It was only two blocks away, so he thanked her for the information, left the van, and decided to enjoy the morning. It was a good time to walk off a little breakfast, and take a look at his new city.

Portage Lake, a deep water river once used to transport copper ore, divided the Keweenaw from the rest of the Upper Peninsula. It was now just a scenic waterway separating Hancock and Houghton with miles of rocky crags, towering pines, and shimmering waters to add to its beauty. Johnny walked from Quincy Street down towards the water feeling the cool mist rising to meet him. Ten minutes later he found the house he was looking for. There on a corner lot sat a little white house with dark green shutters. Directly across the street was a yellow galvanized railing and a forty foot drop down to Portage Lake. He had to go look over the edge imagining what a piece of property with a view like this would cost down in his home town of Grand Rapids. He turned back and looked at the small framed wooden houses on this block and wondered how they survived the terrible snow storms that would roll in off of Lake Superior in the coming months.

Johnny crossed the street, climbed the four steps and rang the bell. The door slowly opened and a short curly permed hairdo attached to a grandmotherly face poked her head out into the frosty air. Replete with a flowered house coat and muffy slippers, he could see the madam of the house wasn't expecting anyone this time of the morning. She reminded him of one of the old live-in aunts, or housekeepers from the early sixties sitcoms, who was slouchy, yet comfortable, but capable and wise to all situations under her roof.

"Good morning Mrs. Aho," (Ayho) he smiled trying to project more confidence than he felt at the moment.

"Aho." (Aaho) was the gruff reply emphasizing the long A. She seemed rather unpleasant as she poked her head out looking in each direction to see if he was alone.

"Aho, yes Mrs. Aho. How are you this morning?" he offered lamely wishing he could go down the steps and start over again.

"What do you want?" she asked pulling her house coat closer to ward off the cold. She looked back into the house as if she might need reinforcements.

"You know, maybe I should come back at a better time to talk about renting the building on Quincy Street," he offered apologetically.

"Nonsense, come in, it's cold out there," she said as she held the door open for him like a barn cat seeing a mouse at the door.

He made his way through the foyer into the living room trying to imagine how cold it would be in February, as she closed out the cold October air. She offered him a seat on an overstuffed davenport with hand-crocheted end pillows. The room was decorated in the style of the nineteen fifties with flowered wallpaper, and old but solid wooden furniture. The house smelled of wood fire smoke, roasted meat, and Finnish humanity all rolled into one. He would soon find out that most of the older homes on the Keweenaw Peninsula had been heated by wood stoves since the great immigration of the 1840's.

"Are you from Hancock?" She asked.

"No, I drove up yesterday from down-state," he said, making himself comfortable. "I spent last night at the Hancock Motel."

"That place is too expensive," she remarked as if by reflex.

John guessed she has no idea what the cost of any lodging was in the area.

He thought it was a bargain by down-state standards, but quickly concurred with her if for no other reason than to try and seem agreeable.

"Well, I got in late and it was the first place I saw with a "Vacancy" sign.

I was kind of pooped after driving non stop from Grand Rapids, maybe I'll look around tomorrow," he said.

"So, you're staying then, at least for a while," she mused. He took his time examining the room and thought his aunt Gracie would be impressed with the collection of green and pink fancy glassware displayed on all the curio shelves.

"You certainly have a beautiful collection of glassware," he smoozed.

"Where did you hear about the building?" she asked, ignoring the flattery.

"I saw it on the bulletin board down at the Kaleva Bakery on Quincy Street."

"Dey got good bakery eh," she smiled, dropping into her Finnish U.P. dialect, which went right over his head.

Not to be out done, he offered. "Ya, dey do eh," rather impressed with his new bi-cultural affectation. For a moment they smiled at each other.

"Would you like coffee?" she asked all cleverness put aside.

"I'd love some," he replied, and together they made their way through the formal dining room to the kitchen. While he sat in a green plastic chair at the matching Formica table, Mrs. Aho put a teaspoon of Sanka in each cup, sliced up a Povititsa loaf and placed it on the table.

"I think it's time I introduced myself, I'm John Hendricks from down-state in the Grand Rapids area." He smiled quickly declaring a truce between a clever woman, and an out-matched smart aleck.

"Well, my name is Helen, and you're along way from home John Hendricks. What are you doing way up here in Hancock?"

"I'm sort of a missionary," he said toying with the spoon.

Her eyes lifted as if he had just climbed out from behind a bush in darkest Africa.

"A missionary in Hancock?" She asked, more of a question than a statement.

"I guess it sounds a little strange," he said "and maybe missionary isn't the right word to use in this situation. It's sort of a commitment, or a pledge if you will, that I have made to God and some fine people in the Grand Rapids area to try and provide a facility in a community where high school and college aged youths can go to relax, study and communicate with each other to relieve some of the tensions from school or home life."

"Hmm," she mused, "Are you a priest, a minister, or just a regular old missionary?"

"Well. It's kind of a long story," he offered.

She slid her chair back, "Let me get the tea kettle, and you can start from the beginning."

For the next half hour, over weak instant decaf and some excellent homemade coffee-cake, John and Helen swapped life stories. He told her about growing up the son and grandson of Christian Reformed preachers, and she told him of the joys and hardships of a young girl's life in a Finnish-American community. Their ages and cultural differences melted away as he told her about his four years at Cornerstone University, and his undergraduate work in Ministerial and Youth Leadership.

"My dad and grandpa, both John Hendricks' arranged the funding for this mission through their large main stream churches in the Grand Rapids area. Together with their committees to support missions in the continental U.S, they agreed to collectively hear my presentation."

Helen spread a little butter on a slice of Povititsa, and passed it over to John without breaking his train of thought.

"You know for many years, American churches thought the mission to fulfill God's promises were only in foreign countries, never considering that right here in our own back yards there were opportunities to roll up our sleeves and help our own brothers and sisters create better lives for themselves. Many different ethnic and cultural groups from the forgotten native Americans to the poor share croppers in the south have"… he paused.

"Helen," he said quietly.

"Yes, John," she responded.

"Sometimes I get so excited I just get carried away."

"That's okay John, I feel your enthusiasm, but what I can't understand is why here? I mean, why Hancock?" Helen said with a perplexed look on her face. "Look around you, you drove through town this morning, this isn't an Indian reservation out west or some big inner city area. There's no blight; there's no hunger. We're not asking anything from anyone. We've been perfectly fine for over a hundred years without any interference, and I don't think Hancock's ready for some outsiders to come in and try to influence our kids."

Helen, having spent all of her emotion stared at John. "John,"

"Yes, Helen."

"I guess sometimes I get carried away too."

John took a sip of cold coffee. "Maybe getting carried away is a good thing. Maybe what I need is a different perspective of what I'm getting myself into," he offered meekly, wondering if he had shot himself in the foot before he had even got in the door.

"John, may I call you Johnny?" She asked.

"Of course, my mom calls me Johnny."

"Lets slow down and start from the beginning without trying to overthrow the government and rounding up all the citizens. Tell me what you've got in mind."

Grateful for the second chance, he leaned back, folded his hands behind his head, and relaxed. "When I was a senior at Cornerstone, I had this vision of starting a youth mission somewhere in the Upper Peninsula. I could see this small rustic city in the pines with lots of lakes and rivers, and in the center of town a building full of teenagers from different areas, having fun while helping each other at the same time."

Helen smiled at the thought.

"One Saturday morning, I mentioned it to my dad, while he was cutting grass, and he said he remembered the dreams he had had of a mission when he was my age, but the subject dropped, and we never talked about it again."

"You know, that's the way life is." Helen said nodding.

"Well, I graduated, and spent two years taking ministerial and youth training courses trying to figure out which direction I should go in. One evening, dad called."

"Your grandpa's talking about something that might interest you. Come on over, we want to talk to you," he said.

Twenty minutes later, the four of us were sitting at the kitchen table. While mom poured coffee, grandpa said that the subject of mission's money had been raised between the two churches. Dad had mentioned that young Johnny had recently proposed a plan for a mission in the Upper Peninsula."

Johnny looked across the table at dad's smirking face. "Well," dad said looking at his son, "we hadn't hammered out anything definite, but you and I had discussed it in general terms."

"Johnny," grandpa said, "you know you have the credentials and backing of both of our congregations, not to mention the loving pride and enthusiasm of your whole family, but the next step is up to you. If you would like to send a written proposal for a youth mission in the U.P., our combined councils will consider it and offer you an opportunity to make a presentation."

Johnny looked at Helen reflecting on that evening, "Well, I made the presentation, and the vote was close, but in the end, they gave me a shot, and here I am. Of course, if I mess up, it's back to Grand Rapids with my tail between my legs. Pretty scary, huh."

I'd say that's a big responsibility for someone coming right out of college. It seems like it would be a lot easier to go somewhere and goof off for a while. I think you've probably earned a break," Helen said.

"You know, I've always been the big brother, the guy who always stayed back to help somebody who wasn't quite keeping up. I spent my whole life watching my folks and grandparents lead by example, and leaning heavily on the Bible. Sounds kind of hokey, I know, but those good folks helped make life a lot better for a lot of people and I guess that's what I'd like to do with my life."

"That sounds pretty ambitious for someone twice your age," she said, "but why did you choose Hancock, and why so far from home?"

"One of my instructors at Cornerstone was born and raised in Laurium not too far north of here. He told me that while he was growing up, there weren't too many organizations or places that took much interest in the local kids. Unless you played hockey, no one noticed you. So, I thought with Michigan Tech on the Houghton side of the Portage River Entry, and Finlandia University in Hancock, plus all of the high school kids in both cities, it would be a perfect place to start a… well, to start a youth mission," he said positively. "It could be a place where kids could come to relax and talk, and maybe just hang out, or shoot a game of pool."

"I can see the look in your eyes that tells me this is not a passing whim, but something much deeper. I'm proud to meet you, Brother John. Maybe we should take a look at that old falling down building you're interested in and see if it's what you have in mind."

Helen covered the coffee cake, put the cups in the sink, and told me to wait in the living room. It only took a moment for her to get dressed, grab her coat, and the key to the building. As they walked up the hill to Quincy Street, Johnny decided that he could get used to this northern hospitality.

Hancock was founded by the Quincy Mining Company in 1859, and Quincy Street became the commercial spine along which all of the support industries took root. The town was built and rebuilt, and like most successful boom towns, it finally developed some real permanency in the early 1900's. The Aho building was erected in that proud era, but today stood in obvious disrepair. Johnny tried not to show his disappointment as he stared through the filthy front window.

"Let's make sure this is the right one," Helen said as she slid the old fashioned skeleton key into the lock. It took some twisting and turning to drive it into the rusted slot, and with great effort, the cylinder finally turned. "Don't expect too much," she said, ducking a cobweb, and kicking an old Coke bottle across the dusty floor.

The musty smell was almost overpowering. "When was the last time you were in here?" Johnny asked trying to get a measure of the place.

"It's been a few years," she said looking up at the shadowy tin type ceiling. "After my husband Arvin died, I didn't like coming up here alone." Her voice seemed to be swallowed up by the emptiness of the room. She seemed to shrink in stature the further we progressed. "I guess there were too many memories."

"Are there any lights?" Johnny asked, catching his toe on an old rolled up carpet.

"I suppose so," she said, "but I had them shut off the electricity years ago. Arvin's dad started a small appliance store after World War Two, hoping to get rich from the returning troops. He had a contract with Westinghouse, and was sure he could sell new stoves and fridges to the homecoming heroes."

It was hard to imagine there was ever any hustle and bustle in this old tomb.

"In all fairness," she reminisced, "he did pretty well, but then the competition moved in across the Lake in Houghton. He kept ordering on credit to keep up with them, but finally the pressure reached its boiling point. One afternoon, my mother in law walked into the store and there he was, lying next to a hand dolly. He was trying to move a refrigerator by himself. They said it was an aneurism."

Standing next to her, Johnny sensed the story had been told many times before.

"Anyway," she sighed, flicking some dirt off her cuff, "up steps Arvin with no experience in running a business; no common sense; too much education; and up to his eyeballs in debt. What could I say? He felt he owed his parents something."

It surprised Johnny how that empty building had brought back so many memories for Helen. He let her go on.

"Arvin and I got married while this was all going on, and to tell the truth, I wasn't much help. A year later our son Steven was on the way. It was tough back then. Everyone was pretending things were getting better, but at the end of the week, there was never enough money to pay all the bills. I'm not saying it was a bad life, but there was no spark. There was never that joy that you expect when you work so hard. On Sunday morning it was easier to pass up the collection basket at church than to embarrass yourselves by putting a few coins in the envelope," she shamefully recalled.

"How did he die?" Johnny asked quietly.

"Mr. Saarinen from the shoe repair across the street found him sitting in his chair, slumped over a pile of unpaid bills." Helen blew her nose into a Kleenex, "It was a sad day standing graveside at the Keweenaw Memorial Cemetery next to little Stevie as Father Bernard sent my Arvin on to heaven. They said it was a heart attack, but I say he died from a broken heart. Lord, he had such dreams. He and Stevie were going to run the business together and the three of us were going to do so many things, and go so many places." She stood quietly staring at an old calendar on the wall from another age.

"Helen, I'm very sorry for your loss," Johnny said, as he slowly eased her towards the light from the front door.

"I've seen enough, I know we can work something out to satisfy both of us. Let's go over to Kaleva's and seal this deal with some good bakery, eh."

Helen led the way out, locked the door, and after a thorough brushing off of shoulders and sleeves, they walked arm in arm up the street to the coffee shop. She soon found her composure as they found a booth by the window, and ordered some thimbleberry pie and coffee.

"Have you had thimbleberry pie before?" She asked, as a waitress set the two slices of the red berry pie covered with whip cream, in front of them.

"They look like raspberries," he said.

"Hold your voice down, or you'll get us both thrown out of here," Helen said hushing Johnny. "There are very few places in the world these very special berries grow, and the Keweenaw Peninsula just happens to be one of them."

"And what makes them so special?" Johnny asked sarcastically.

"Well, they're much larger, and tastier," she paused, and they're also softer," she said enthusiastically. "They can't be shipped commercially except as jams and jellies, so," she said dramatically, "you have the unique pleasure of eating fresh thimbleberry pie right here at Kaleva's. Ta Da." She said with a flourish, winking at the waitress.

He noticed that Helen had drawn the attention of all the locals in the neighboring booths and that they had their eyes on him as his fork sliced down through the fluffy whipped cream into the sacred berries.

"Yuuuuuumm." He proclaimed, smacking his lips, much to the delight of everyone within ear shot, and especially his new friend Helen. While he enjoyed this Keweenaw delicacy, he also observed that there was a oneness about this group of people who were bound together by financial and physical hardships, as well as a pride in who they were and where they came from.

He knew that this observation would be important in dealing with all the citizens of Hancock in the future. With enthusiasm he and Helen discussed the building and possible mission and in the end, they both agreed that it was worth pursuing. Helen said that money wasn't an issue, but that he needed to go to Hancock City Hall and find out what he had to do to legally open the building. As they left the bakery, Helen walked home while Johnny crossed the street toward City Hall. It seemed like things couldn't be going any better on this beautiful sunny morning.

CHAPTER 2

The Hancock Town Hall and Fire Station was built in 1899. It was a two story facility with a ninety foot tall clock tower all made out of sand stone dragged from the quarry near Jacobsville, twenty miles away. Today, City Hall is on the second floor overlooking Quincy Street with the offices and the city commission meeting room looking much the same as they did a century ago.

Ignoring the elevator, and taking the well worn steps to the second floor, Johnny was greeted by a pleasant woman in a bright print dress with "Penny Wolfston" printed on her name tag.

"Good afternoon, may I help you?"

"My name is John Hendricks, and I'm planning on renting the old Aho building down the street. I want to know what I need to do to open a mission."

"What's a mission?" she politely asked.

"I want to open a Christian Mission for the youth of Hancock," He said.

"Well, who do you represent then?" she queried.

"Jesus Christ," he replied as sincerely as possible.

"Just one minute," she replied and with the look of a bank teller who had just been handed a note from a robber, hastened to the back of the office.

After a short conference between Penny and a couple of officious looking public servants, the three approached Johnny with a somber forbearing.

"Good afternoon," said the senior officiate. "Ms. Wolfston tells me you're interested in renting the old Aho building on Quincy."

"Yes"

"And the purpose of your business?" he asked.

"I want to open up a mission for the young people in Hancock." Johnny replied.

"And you are representing whom?" The man volleyed back.

"As I told the young lady, I would like to open a Christian Youth Mission for the youth in the Houghton-Hancock area. You do believe in Jesus Christ don't you?" Johnny asked somewhat piqued.

"Well of course I do, we all do, everybody does, well not everybody, but you know what I mean," the public official blustered.

"Well, I'm sure everything will be fine then. If you will please tell me what I need to do to bring the old building up to code I can get started."

"Slow down a little Mr. Hendricks, I know it all seems easy to you, but there are certain rules and procedures we have to follow for you and Mrs. Aho to start the resurrection of this very old and historical building. We will contact her and begin the process and when that is finished, we will discuss what you intend on doing with the building. I do hope that this will all fit in with your plans," he said curtly.

"I'll be in touch," Johnny said wishing he had handled the situation a little better.

"Eh, Mr. Hendricks, do you have an address you can be reached at." Ms. Wolfston asked as he turned to leave.

"I'll be in touch," he repeated as he exited city hall with all eyes piercing his back. What had started out as a great day had suddenly fallen apart? As he headed for his van, it was evident that the only friends he seemed to have in the U.P. were Helen and God.

He parked across from Helen's and climbed the steps feeling like he'd lost a precious gift he had been entrusted to watch. How many times had he been told in his young life that he was responsible for everything that came out of his mouth?

"Come in, Come in," Helen said warmly, "sit down on the sofa. I'm all ears. Tell me, what did they say?"

"Well," he meekly answered, "I'm not sure, but I think I made a bad impression. I thought they would share my enthusiasm, but they treated me like a foreigner."

"You are a foreigner, Johnny. I should have gone with you. People in Hancock are very conservative. You had no way of knowing what this area has been through. Most folks in Michigan don't even know we're here. We're a place to camp in the summer, hunt in the fall, and talk about how bad the weather is the rest of the year. We're called "Yoopers" by you good folks down below the "Big Mac Bridge", disrespected and ignored. Look in the local news paper. There are few job opportunities, and want ads are mostly for used snow mobiles and chain saws. Folks up here don't think like you, and we don't understand you."

"I don't know what to say." Johnny said.

"Well, I do," Helen said. "I need to introduce you to a few people to give you a better understanding of how things are. Where are you staying tonight?"

"The Motel, I guess."

"Cancel," she snapped as if she were the captain of a ship. "We're not wasting anymore money on motels when I've got a guest room right here."

"You have a guest room?" He asked.

"Yes, it was my son's room a long time ago."

"Where does he live now?" Johnny asked curiously.

"Well, we lost him a while back, and the room is available. You go to the Motel and get your things, and I'll make up the bed. It'll be fine, you just wait and see."

With that she rushed him to the door and said, "Don't be late for supper."

As he slowly walked down to his car, his mind told him, Quick get in your car and head for home. There are lots of things you can do and places you can go without all these headaches. This was a mistake. You can do better. Run. Run.

As he slid behind the wheel shaking from the cold, he mused, "God, I don't want to do this. Get somebody else. There are lots of people who are better at this than I am," And then he lay down on his front seat and cried for the first time since he was a boy. With the tears misting in his eyes, and his body shaking from the cold, he began laughing uncontrollably. "John," he thought "you are a turkey. God didn't bring you all the way up here so that you could have a hissy fit. Go get your stuff," he laughed. "You are not alone. You are the worker and God is the Boss. Go get your stuff."

All the way to the motel, he tried to concoct a story so he wouldn't have to pay for another nights lodging. When he approached the desk an attractive young lady, probably a coed from one of the Universities smiled and said,

"Mrs. Aho just called and explained the situation,"

"You know Helen?"

"Yes, we're neighbors; I'm Jenny Parvuu, three houses down on the left. I can see by your card that your name is John, and you're from Grand Rapids. I've always wanted to visit down-state, but here I am trapped above the bridge."

It was nice to talk to someone close to his age, and he had a lot of questions to ask, but she shut him off quickly.

"Helen said not to waste time chatting, there is plenty of time for that. Hurry back up the hill, supper's on the table," Jenny said imitating Helen's voice perfectly.

Johnny loaded up his things and returned the key to Jenny.

"If it's okay, I've got a million questions about Hancock and the surrounding area. Would it be okay if maybe tomorrow sometime we could talk?"

"I'd love to," she smiled, "Here's my phone number."

The temperature had dropped another ten degrees as he left the motel, but Johnny had a warm feeling inside that he hadn't had for a while. When he arrived back at the house, Helen had the front porch light on, and he felt like he was really home. It had been a long day, and the prospect of moving into a new place and maybe starting a new life was a little unsettling. But, with all the excitement and confusion he had faced today, he knew that Helen had a plan, and God had his back. Johnny knew he would sleep like a baby tonight.

The next morning, seated across from Helen at the kitchen table, they began to hatch out a plan.

"Up here we don't talk about Jesus like he is the CEO of some new corporation. We all have different ways of dealing with our individual faiths, and people in City Hall won't be bullied by yours. Bringing a sledge hammer to introduce yourself to the leaders of the community you hope to live and succeed in seems a little brash," Helen offered sarcastically with a grin.

"You know, I just blew it. They're not even going to want to talk to me let alone understand what I want to try to do. What a mess I've made of things."

"The sun doesn't rise and set on Hancock Michigan, and one little mistake is not the end of the world," pontificated Helen.

Just then, Jenny with her blond hair pulled back in a ponytail stuck her head in the back door and asked, "Is the coffee still hot?"

"Come in, come in Jenny, have a seat and I'll get you a cup," said Helen. "Our crusader from down-state needs a little cheering up."

"What happened?" asked Jenny reaching for the sugar.

"Well, I shot off my big mouth on my first day in town."

"Johnny had some words with Bob Heikinen down at City Hall, just a misunderstanding." Helen interjected. "No problem at all."

"Is that the Bob Heikinen that sits two rows down from us at the 9:00 A.M. Mass?"

"Ya, Dorothy's husband from Tuesday night Bible study." said Helen.

"He's kind of a jerk, I think," said Jenny smiling at Johnny supportively.

This is going to turn into a bigger mess than it already is, John mused. These two ladies are going to get me run out of town.

"Maybe there's a better way in dealing with this than calling him names," Johnny said.

"I've got a better idea, why don't you two go out and have breakfast and I'll make a few phone calls? After all, Bob wanted to talk to me anyway. Now leave me to my specialty."

"What's her specialty?" asked Johnny as Jenny escorted him towards his van."

"Community relations," Jenny smiled taking Johnny by the arm.

Houghton, the largest city in the area, is the sister city of Hancock on the south shore of the Portage Lake, with a bustling downtown area and Michigan Technological University in its midst. He and Jenny parked the van on Main Street and entered a student haunt called "The Copper Rail". They found a table near the baked goods and threw their coats over the backs of their chairs. Business was brisk which added to the savior faire, and they couldn't have been happier.

"What do you do besides run the hottest motel in Hancock?" John asked reaching for a donut with chocolate sprinkles on it.

"Well, I'm a full time student at Tech, and I work at WMTU's radio station." said Jenny pouring two coffees, and snagging a fruit tart.

"You're kidding." Johnny said, as he paid the bill and toted the tray to the table.

"Yes sir, I'm a registered D.J. on weekends for college credits."

"I'm impressed, how'd you get the gig?" He asked losing half the sprinkles down the front of his shirt.

"My ex boyfriend was the senior class rep for the station, and they needed a couple of underclassmen to man the boards, so, I volunteered."

"And what do you do for fun?" John asked like a television interviewer.

"I usually pick up strange guys at the local motel," she said pertly, breaking off the corner of her tart and licking out the prune filling.

"Well, I sure hope you have discriminating taste," John said.

"My friends tell me I don't, but who knows," she replied with a wink.

They finished their coffee, and Jenny said, "Come on, I'll show you the big city."

As they went through the campus area, he wondered why he hadn't picked Houghton as a destination for his mission, and the answer was obvious. He didn't pick Hancock; God did. They found a bench down by the waterway and watched the sailboats glide down the lake.

"Did you ever meet Helen's son?" Johnny asked casually.

"Why do you ask?"

"Oh, Helen told me I could stay in his room, and I don't know, it just seemed strange. I mean, did he leave, or did he die, or was he killed or something?"

Johnny was in uncharted waters and hoped his question hadn't open up a bad memory. He was feeling like an outsider again.

"I don't know much about it. It was before I was born. It had something to do with Viet Nam. He was a soldier and something happened. I don't know what. Anyway it was back in the seventies, and he's buried by his dad." Jenny informed him.

Once again, he had inexplicably opened up another personal memory which was none of his business and it made him feel uncomfortable.

"Helen doesn't talk about it, and I guess I'm too young to be much help to her emotionally. She's always been kind of a quiet friend from church. Whenever someone has a problem, she always finds a way to help," Jenny said.

There was a lull in the conversation as they soaked up the sun.

"Father down at church says she's an angel. I know she's sure nice to me. She's kind of like a second mom. I know you're worried about the folks down at City Hall, but count on Helen to figure out a way to fix it."

"Let's go back and see what she's up to," he said.

The late October sun shone like diamonds on the water as they crossed the lift bridge heading into Hancock. There was a feeling of togetherness as they drove up the hill with a Beachboys tune jamming on the oldies program from across the lake on WMTU radio.

"Thank you, Bob," Helen said, hanging up the telephone as Johnny and Jenny walked through the door.

"Was that my buddy from City Hall?" Johnny asked, already embarrassed by my own flippancy.

"It certainly was," Helen replied ignoring his callous response. "Bob wants to meet with us this afternoon at about 3:00. I'm sure we can smooth things out and make a fresh start."

"What do I need to do?" Johnny asked feeling insecure again.

"You can start by putting on some more businesslike clothes," Helen said. "You'll be dealing with an elected representative who has earned the respect of the citizens of this city. The least we can do is show him the same respect. Your mission is to help the youth of this city, not to join them. This may be your only chance to make things right. Don't throw it away with your immaturity. I know your father and mother are expecting a bigger effort as well."

The kitchen was suddenly quiet as the full responsibility of who he was and what his mission was fell directly on his shoulders. Who in the world did he think he was? With four eyes staring at him, he felt like a little boy being scolded by his grade school teacher. He then turned to the only One in his life with the power to forgive and to bless. He held out his hands to Helen and Jenny, and as they responded, he bowed his head…

> *"Dear Father, forgive me for being such a fool. You have granted me a great opportunity to help others through You, and instead, I am so full of myself, that I am jeopardizing all You have given me. You have blessed me with friendship and loyalty. I promise to try and be worthy of both. Help me to do your work Father, Amen."*

There was an aura of togetherness as they squeezed each other's hands, and he said in a quiet voice, "I'm going to go take a shower, I've got work to do."

"Call me when you get back," Jenny said on her way out the door, "and good luck."

Johnny held the front door to City Hall as he and Helen made their way to the information desk, and Ms. Wolfston was waiting.

"Hi Helen, Mr. Heikinen is waiting, I'll tell him you're here." Penny said.

"Thanks Penny," Helen responded.

"Helen it's nice to see you," Bob said as he ushered them into his office. The area though small, held all the mementoes of an involved public servant, with the obvious trapping of a lifetime of community service. Bob was well liked and respected in Hancock.

"John," Bob said holding out his hand, "it's nice to see you too. I think we got off on the wrong foot yesterday, but I'm sure we can straighten this out. Please, both of you have a seat. John, I'm sure Helen told you we discussed the Aho building, and its structural condition, as well as its value to the historical district. The first is obvious, the building hasn't been used for a long time, and the city needs to get in there and inspect the wiring, water pipes, and indeed, the overall safety of the entire facility before we can let anyone in there to do anything. I'm sure you understand that."

Johnny nodded quietly.

"The second part is a little more difficult to understand." Bob tapped a pencil on his desk, and then stopped. "The city of Hancock began as a copper mining camp around 1859. As the area grew and prospered, a town developed to fulfill the needs of the miner. We are presently sitting on the land where the Quincy mine opened, and everything, including this street and most of the buildings on it make up a national historical district. As elected officials, the city council has a responsibility to protect all of the assets under our charter and to ensure that the customs and traditions of the Finnish American community are protected. Does that make sense, John?"

He nodded once again, and Bob went on.

"Is there anything that you can tell me about your life, and who you represent that would help me to understand exactly what your plans might be to help ingratiate you to our community?"

"First, Mr. Heikinen, I would like to deeply apologize, for my behavior, and my attitude yesterday. I'm sure a lack of sleep and too much adrenalin made me look very foolish." He looked at Helen. "I will apologize to Ms. Wolfston when we leave." John paused to collect himself. "I am a third generation John Hendricks. My dad's grandparents came from the Netherlands and he and my grandfather are both pastors of large Christian Reformed churches in the Grand Rapids area. They have dedicated their lives to serving the Lord, and I have chosen to follow in their footsteps. My mother, Angelina Hendricks, was born in Mexico and walked across the border at San Diego with her sister, and never looked back. Through the help of family and friends, they caught a cross country bus to western Michigan where relatives put them up, and found housekeeping jobs for them."

Johnny paused for a moment and cleared his throat.

"My aunt soon married a citizen, but my mother studied English and entered high school. She met my dad at a Christian youth rally in downtown Grand Rapids. Needless to say, when dad brought his new illegal Mexican friend to Sunday dinner, the conversation was a little stilted. Grandpa not suspecting that love was in the air asked Angie questions about her life, and what her plans were. When mom told her story, everyone listened intently."

"What would you like to do with your life, Angelina?" Grandpa asked.

"I must help my people who are trapped in your country who won't go home, and are not welcome here," she replied looking around the table.

"And where are these lost souls?" Grandpa asked.

"All around your beautiful city working any entry level job they can get."

You could have heard a pin drop. Two years later, dad and mom tied the knot in Grandpa's church, and moved into the inner city where they had me. They spent the next five years building a church that not only taught the mercy of God, but also taught adults to read and write, and to embrace the freedoms we have. That's where I come from, sir. I spent the first seven years of my life helping feed, play with and change Latino baby diapers." I smiled. "At age five, my Spanish was as good as my English. The gift of sharing and co-operating were ingrained in every part of my life. Grandpa helped dad organize and fund an Anglo Latino Community Church with all kinds of classes and community activities seven days a week. Mother spent long hours every day helping our neighborhood friends adapt to a new way of life. I started kindergarten at an inner city school at the age of five, and spent most of my time defending myself and my Latino friends from poor black and white kids who finally had a new minority to challenge.

But, as tired as mom, dad, and I were at the end of the day, we always thanked God for the opportunity He gave us to share His love. I followed the straight and narrow the Bible tells us about with my eyes on the horizon and God at my back." He stopped to catch his breath.

"Can I hear an Amen," Helen said to break the spell.

"I'm sorry," Johnny said. "Sometimes I get carried away. I finished college last spring, and the family council decided my best course of action would be a field mission away from home to try and give youth in an economically stressed area a place to hang out and find themselves. I have been charged with that duty and am fully funded by the congregations of two of the biggest churches in southwest Michigan. We are not interested in converting or changing anyone. I promise to work with all the churches, civic organizations and any ethnic cultures in the area. A friend from college who grew up here told me about the economic dependency of the mining industry in the past, and the need to listen to youth to help them find their way. Just consider me an extra pair of hands to assist our local kids to get through the toughest period of their lives."

He stopped to the sound of Bob rhythmically tapping a pencil on the edge of his desk.

"John, that was quite a presentation, and I think I'm beginning to understand where you're coming from, but I have to be frank with you. I spoke with some of the council members this morning before our meeting, and it's going to be an uphill battle. The council gave me the power to nix your project right here and now. I probably shouldn't have told you that because I've decided to let you make your presentation before the whole council. It only seems fair to let you know what you're up against."

Bob leaned forward, folded his hands, and looked John in the eyes.

"This is a small community, and the little scene you created here yesterday was all over town before you got back to Helen's. There has been a political war between Lansing and the U.P. for a long time, and anything done or offered from below the Bridge, is looked on with suspicion. You're lucky to have a strong ally in Helen, but believe me these negative feelings run deep throughout this community. So, I hope you will understand if the council goes against you. We are very slow to change and try anything new. Sometimes we make good decisions and everyone is pleased, but other times we have been taken advantage of by choosing projects without enough background information. If it means anything, I'll be on your side, but I can't promise anything. The council will meet next Wednesday at 7:30 p.m. in the city commission room, and you will have a chance to propose your project. I wish you the best."

They all stood up, shook hands and while Helen chatted with Bob, Johnny made his way up front to apologize to Penny.

Outside the building, the wind had picked up, and the heavy dark clouds blowing in off of Lake Superior seemed like an omen of things to come. Helen came through the front door.

"Johnny, I'm so proud of you. It took a lot of courage to say the things you felt, and I'm sure Bob could see it was from your heart." Helen said, taking his arm to help block the wind.

"Thanks, Helen, I couldn't have done it without your support, but right now I've got to call my folks and let them know what's going on. Head over to Kaleva's and save us a booth, and I'll meet you in a few minutes."

"Hello," Angie said, recognizing Johnny's number on her phone.

"Hi mom, it's your prodigal son in beautiful downtown Hancock, and believe it or not, I think it's starting to snow," he said laughingly.

"You've got to be kidding, Honey, did you have a good trip?" She asked.

"Yeah, it was smooth sailing all the way," Johnny tucked into a doorway to get out of the weather. "I even made a couple of contacts in town."

"Did you find a room?"

"Better than that, I moved from a motel to a private residence with an extra bedroom. Mom, my landlady's name is Mrs. Aho and she owns a building in downtown Hancock that would be perfect for a youth mission."

"You're staying in a mission?"

"No, I'm staying in her home. She is a widow and is renting me the guest room in her house. It's a perfect situation. I can stay there, and she can rent me her building for a mission."

"Tell me about the building, dear."

"There are a few conditional problems I can remedy, and of course electrical and plumbing inspections, but the biggest obstacle is that the city council has to approve the idea of a faith-supported mission in the heart of the historical district."

"That doesn't sound like a problem. Have you talked to anybody?"

"That's the real problem mom. I may have jinxed the whole project by putting my foot in my mouth."

"Okay, okay, slow down. Start from the beginning and tell me everything."

I felt a certain comfort in talking to my mom, and for the next fifteen minutes I related the odyssey of the last two days. It wasn't easy laying out my shortcomings to the woman who had taught me better, but in the end, I realized that complete candor was the only way to solicit help from the home front.

"And you say the meeting is Wednesday night?"

"Yes at 7:30 in City Hall."

"I'm going to talk to you're dad and grandpa and we'll call you tomorrow. Don't worry Honey, together we'll figure this out."

"Bye, mom thanks for the support. I love you."

"Good bye dear. I love you, too."

As he crossed the street, the wind seemed to have died down a little. He felt such hope yesterday, why had everything turned so sour?

It was quiet around the dinner table as Angie related Johnny's story to dad and grandpa.

"It could be nothing at all," dad said, "probably a misunderstanding. You know how boys his age can blow things out of proportion. I think maybe we should let things run their course, and see what happens. If he comes running for help every time there's a bump in the road, he won't learn how to solve problems or stand on his own feet."

"That's an excellent point, son," grandpa offered, "but I think there's something deeper here that we should investigate. We certainly learned a lot about ethnic differences in our own city, and I must confess we weren't very quick to accept and adjust to them. It seems this Finnish American community might be similar to our local Latino population, and I'm sure you remember the obstacles we faced by assuming they thought like we did."

"A point well taken, dad, maybe I should call Mr. Heikinen this evening, and see if I can get a little broader picture of the situation. I don't want to interfere, but Johnny did ask for our advice."

"Good evening, this is John Hendricks. Could I speak with Robert Heikinen, please?"

"Just a minute," a young voice answered. "Dad," she hollered into another room.

"Hello," Bob answered.

"John Hendricks, Mr. Heikenen, calling from down state. How are you this evening?"

"Fine, may I call you John?"

"If I can call you Bob," John said good naturedly.

"It's a deal. I suppose this is about the meeting I had with you're son this afternoon."

"You know, Bob, I'm kind of embarrassed to call. I know Johnny's pretty good at making a fool of himself, his father is a professional at it, and if I'm out of line, I'll butt out, but..."

"John," Bob interrupted, "your son did a great job of presenting his vision this afternoon, and if it were up to me alone, I would seriously consider it, but there are some members of the town council who are against it. Howard Berg, the leader of the opposition, thinks his ancestors discovered the Keweenaw, and he has a following that always backs him. He holds a lot of power as the Chairman of the Historical District, and that means a lot because tourism is the only thing that draws outsiders to Hancock."

"You know, Bob, I think we may have acted before we had a chance to study what an outside mission might do to your city. I apologize for not getting more involved before sending Johnny up there. Maybe, we should reconsider the idea. I certainly didn't intend to put my son in a situation where he had no chance of succeeding."

"Hold on John, the mission isn't the problem, I think we could convince the council and the people of Hancock that there is a need for a place for young people to gather that is supervised by a certified youth leader, better yet, an interfaith leader. That is something we can present to the community. If we promote the project in the newspaper, maybe we'll get some citizens to show up for the meeting on Wednesday evening."

"Bob, I think that's more than fair. We'll put our heads together down here, and see if we can add something to the presentation. Thank you for speaking with me and sharing your view. I'm sure that the City of Hancock is in good hands through your leadership. Good night, Bob, and God bless you."

John turned the phone off and went into the kitchen to relay the news to Angie.

"Let's sleep on it and we'll talk to grandpa in the morning," she said.

CHAPTER 3

R.J. Hackala

The street light hanging over the corner of 7th and Blanch Street in Houghton had been shot by an errant BB gun many weeks ago. This hillside area south of town was mostly populated by students from Michigan Tech, known as "Techies" by the general population. The lone light from the upstairs neighbor's window would work nicely. The three teenagers furtively hunkered next to the late model Ford Truck, were doing everything in their power to blend in with the darkness. It was R.J.Hackala, of course, who was in charge of this particular sortie, but then, he was always in charge, and Ben Ryan, Joe Kaufanen were powerless to do anything but follow him through one heist after another.

Actually, this wasn't the first time that R.J. and his two pals squatted next to this particular vehicle. It was only the night before that they had been here to steal the original battery. It was tossed in a dumpster on their way home last night, and tonight was the *coup de grace*. In a few minutes, they would extract the new battery and cables only purchased today at the Super Walmart. With pen light ready, the three thieves rose to quietly lift the hood.

"All right, let's stand up nice and easy fellas." Officer Danny Johnson said, as he pointed his eighteen inch flash light directly into the eyes of the stunned R.J. Hackala.

'We weren't doin nuthin," uttered a shaken Ben Ryan.

Joe chimed in with a dispassionate, "yeah you cops are always pickin on us 'cause we don't go to yer stupid school no more."

R.J. rose slowly with a half smirk on his face.

The revolving beacon on top of the squad car had managed to shine in nearly all of the bed room windows in the neighborhood, and it wasn't long before a crowd gathered to see justice in action.

After the cuffs were secured, and a little neighborly name calling ensued, Officer Johnson assisted the three reprobates into the rear seat of the cruiser. The well-lit City of Houghton seemed quieter than usual as Danny slowly made his way down to U.S. 41 taking a left at MTU. There was a certain sense of satisfaction knowing that he was a source of positive growth in the area. With the University growing every year, and tourism a year-round industry, it wouldn't be long before he might even pick up another stripe. Folks around the state called it the Copper Country, but those days were long since past.

The three teens in the back seat sat in silence as they passed the row of fraternity houses on their way into downtown Houghton. The expression on R.J.'s face gave no clue as to the anger raging deep inside. Through a twisted and fractious upbringing, he never quite understood society's position. As far back as he could remember, people were always there to stop or take away the life and values he was raised with. God had made this beautiful country for everyone to enjoy, not just the ones who sat in the big buildings and made their laws to stop the common man from earning a living.

Danny drove past the court house to the lock-up, and as he stopped the car, he caught R.J.'s eyes in the rear view mirror, flashing him one of his quixotic smiles.

As they passed single file through the station, Danny said to the desk sergeant, "Look who I found stealing a battery up on Blanch and 7th Street. You know, catching bad guys is like fishing, if you never catch any, it ain't much fun."

"You got that right," said Officer Ron Burch, behind the desk. "We'll have to call Howard Berg in the morning, over in Hancock, and tell him we've picked up his nephew R.J. again. He's going to be tickled about that."

"You know we ought to lock up the kid's mother when we pick him up," said Danny.

"Well, this time old R.J. is heading for Escanaba to spend some time at the Bay Pines Youth Detention Camp. Let's see how Uncle Howard likes that. I don't think it'll do much for his political career," Burch said. "I think the folks in Hancock have heard enough about his sister-in-law Kitty to keep the gossip going until next election."

"We'll see." Danny said as he made his way towards the detention cells. "Sleep tight, boys, we'll have you arraigned right after breakfast."

R.J. on the top bunk rolled on his side with his back to the hall light, and tried to figure out his next move. He was sure that as soon as the cops called his mother, she would call Uncle Howard. She'd be mad because after tending bar until 1:00 at Rudy's bar on Quincy, she'd be tired and hung over when the phone rang. Kitty and Howard would have their usual tiff as to who was to blame, and what to do about her kid. R.J. rolled over on his back and stared at the ceiling and wondered what the jail would serve for breakfast. Actually R.J. was making good money fencing stolen auto parts to Victor down in Baraga, and as long as he kept his kid brother straight, and in school, he was doing fine. He could do some community service or pay a fine, and be back in business tomorrow. Life had its ups and downs, but he was doing all right.

The phone rang twice on the desk of Howard Berg's Insurance Agency. He put down his coffee cup and said "Berg Insurance, Howard speaking," into his speaker phone.

Howard Berg was born in Laurium, an old copper mining town, and the home of the Calumet Heckla Mine. His father was the manager of ore processing and was considered a prominent town leader. Howard was raised in an era when excellence and hard work was rewarded. The less ambitious, namely the idled miners who had lost their jobs, were looked down on. Howard, a tall, rangy young man with an ever present crew cut, had his dad's ambition, and was well liked by the upper echelon of the retired mining hierarchy. While the community was languishing, he managed to turn a few good ideas into money and started up the Berg Insurance Company. Going door to door, he built up the largest Independent Agency in Houghton County. When things slowed in Laurium, he moved to Hancock, opened up a new office, and married Margaret Dunne. They were unable to have children, and Howard soon got restless and lost his enthusiasm for work. Local politics became the salve that healed his boredom. With his friends and connections, in the business world, as well as his community and church associations, he soon began to focus on everything in Hancock but his business. Howard became the big fish in the small pond in Hancock, and he loved it. Maggie, as he called his wife, kept house and spent most of her free time with her sister Kitty and her boys R.J. and Jimmy. Kitty was a single mom whose husband, Robert, had deserted them. Working nights, and sleeping days, had sapped her of all her energy, and two teenage boys were more than she could handle.

"Yo, Howard, Tom Meade, Houghton P.D." the officer said. "We picked up your nephew R.J. last night, with a couple of his buddies stealing a car battery again."

"For God sakes Tommy, don't you guys have anything better to do than chase kids around at night?"

"You know, Howard, we've gone pretty easy on R.J., but this time I'm afraid we're going to have to send him down to Escanaba. This is the third time we picked him up for petty larceny, and he doesn't seem to ever learn. I'm not completely blaming your sister, but somebody's got to take control of R.J. and his kid brother Jimmy. I know Kitty won't like it, but I think Escanaba might be the place to straighten him out," Tommy said.

"What's this about Jimmy?" Howard asked. "I thought he was doing all right."

"Arthur Schram over at the middle school has him on his truancy list. He says the boy goes in the front door and out the back without even saying hello. Plus, he's a loner. His teacher Mrs. Merkel says he doesn't talk to anyone. She says he's a time bomb waiting to go off. He kind of creeps the other kids out, Howard. Usually those are the ones who get into fights, but he just doesn't care. He's going to be a problem. I hate to bring you more bad news, but he won't stay under the radar much longer."

"I'm sorry Tommy; I appreciate you giving me the heads up on these kids. I'll have to call Kitty and read her the riot act again. You know Tommy we never pulled this kind of crap when we were kids. It's just basic respect.

Nobody teaches that kind of stuff anymore. Don't get me wrong, I know there are lots of good kids out there, but why did I get stuck with two stinkers. And they're not even mine. I'll talk to Kitty and get back to you. See you Thursday night at the Bowling Alley, buddy."

"Yeah, you know me, that's my favorite night of the week."

Howard hung up and called Kitty. The phone rang five times, and the answering machine went on. Beep.

"Kitty, Howard. R.J.'s in jail again and I'm getting sick and tired of the cops calling me instead of you. Get out of bed and run down to the station, and see if you can get him out. You may not be interested in your own reputation, but I've got to live in this city. I'm tired of you and your family dragging me down. By the way, you had better have a talk with your little Jimmy. The school people tell me that he doesn't bother to go to class anymore. Maybe he needs counseling. Maybe you all need counseling. I don't know, but you better do something, because I've had it, and don't go whining to your sister because she's had it too. Goodbye."

Kitty left the phone lying on the bed and rolled over toward the wall, dragging her comforter up over her head to help drive out the pounding headache. She wondered what she had done to deserve this curse that God had placed on her. If the Lord could take her now, this would be the time. She had no reason to live. She hated everything she was, everything she had, and everybody in her life, especially those two ungrateful sons. Why couldn't they live with their father? He had enough money to drink on. He certainly had plenty of time to keep an eye on them. Why was she always the caretaker? If she could just get away, even for a few days, she thought. The sun was a sharp slash across the bottom of the window shade, and she knew it was pointless to lie in bed feeling sorry for her self. Without moving her body, she reached across the bed, grabbed the telephone, pulled it back under the covers, and called the County lock-up.

In a voice as raspy as sand paper, she said, "Good morning, this is Kitty Hackala," her tongue barely able to wrap around the words.

"Ah, good morning to you, Mrs. Hackala," Tom Meade responded, sensing the pain pulsing through the phone. "I suppose this is about your son, R.J."

"Duh" she said, "I understand there's been a little mix up, and once again my son R.J. is stuck in the middle of it. You know I try to keep him away from those other two troublemakers, but it's so hard to keep track of children when you're a single mother and working full time. I can see I'm going to have to try something else, maybe counseling, or a church group or something."

The silence hung in the air after her last sentence. Kitty didn't want to promise too much, and Tommy didn't care.

"Kitty, May I call you Kitty," Tom asked, "I'm afraid the situation has gone well past that. We have R.J. and his friends locked up for committing their third robbery, and he's going to have to be penalized. I would suggest you hire some legal representation and come down to the station."

"I don't think you understand my finances," she shouted into the phone. "If he needs a lawyer, you're going to have to provide one. I'm broke." Click.

CHAPTER 4

Helen and Johnny returned to her house, but there wasn't much to say. He told her about the conversation with his mom, but everything seemed up in the air. He went to his new room and lay down on the bed. The only chance he had to clarify the situation was to write an editorial explaining the merits of a central youth program and placing it in The Mining Gazette by Monday. He wasn't trying to rebuild the Great Wall of China; He only wanted to make life's passage a little easier for some troubled youths. He couldn't help everyone; that was God's job. He just knew there were kids out there who needed someone to listen to them, and he would have the place, the time, and the financial backing. All he needed to do was to convince this group of hard headed conservative council members that the need was there, and he was the man for the job.

Johnny woke up Saturday morning tangled in his blankets, being chased through the streets of Hancock by a group of angry Vikings screaming, "Leave our kids alone." It took a few seconds to get his bearings, and when he heard Helen coming down the hallway, he was awake.

"Johnny, Jenny's on the phone, and wants to know what you're doing this morning." Helen shouted through his door.

"Tell her to come over in a half an hour and we'll go out for breakfast."

They drove north out of Hancock passed the derelict Quincy Mine, which had become the graveyard of rusted metal and abandoned buildings from a century ago. He turned on their favorite radio station and the heater, and drove to Calumet, a city from another era. Beautiful sandstone churches on both sides of the road created a gateway to this one time copper boom town originally called Red Jacket.

"I suppose all the miners wore red jackets," Johnny smirked.

"No, actually Red Jacket was a great Indian chief in the 1830's and was so well respected, that the people honored him by naming the town after him. When you grow up in the Keweenaw, you learn these things," Jenny said with a certain aloofness.

"I don't know how old Chief Red Jacket slipped through the cracks of my southern Michigan education," Johnny chided.

"Stick with me, and I'll do my best to help you catch up with the rest of us. Let's go over to Tony's and buy some pasties, and have a picnic up on Brockway," she said.

"Deal," he said as they headed for Laurium to pick up lunch.

Driving north toward Copper Harbor, he was impressed by the piles of slag stone refuse and the endless pine forests. There was little traffic on either side of the road. The radio reception began to fade so they turned it off.

"What do you think the odds are of the council letting me open the mission," he asked.

"I don't know Johnny, but I think the barrier of doing something new was there before you came to town. It's maddening to think that with all of the people who are twenty five and younger, we are still controlled by a minority of naysayers. Every year, one generation graduates, packs up and moves to a more favorable area of the country to live their lives. If the council stops you, the old timers in town will smile and agree that they have saved the heritage of our proud city. It seems like they have created a museum for their own edification and left the rest of us to wallow in its dust." Jenny said angrily.

"Whoa, slow down little lady," Johnny said in his best John Wayne shtick. "I didn't drive all the way up to the U.P. to let a bunch of hard nosed Yoopers push us around. Can I hear an Amen?"

"Amen, Pardner, and God bless you for coming."

We arrived at Copper Harbor and took a left on M-26 toward Brockway Mountain Drive. One of the original settlers of Copper Harbor was Daniel Brockway, who in the 1840's was instrumental in helping to civilize the area after the ore was discovered, by bringing tourists and miners by boats and canoes.

"Take a left at the next road and put your van in low gear," Jenny advised. "It's very steep and the road isn't always in the best condition."

Brockway Mountain Drive rises 735 feet above Lake Superior, and is a roller coaster ride with sheer precipices falling into valleys of giant conifers on our left.

"What if we meet somebody coming down," he asked firmly gripping the wheel.

"We'll figure something out," she said.

"Oh," was all he could say.

The wind was howling as they reached the parking lot at the summit. The gray clouds scudded past them as they left the van for a better view. Freezing gusts were blasting their faces when Jenny took Johnny's hand to keep from falling. So far, it was the best part of the day.

The white caps far below on Lake Superior, and the infinite horizon helped them to appreciate how insignificant their lives and their worldly problems were. They sat on a massive boulder and watched an iron ore freighter traverse the endless water on its way to Duluth to load up its hold with the iron ore that changed the face of America.

"I'll race you back to the van," Jenny shouted above the wind, and took off running towards the parking lot.

Beating a Keweenaw native on her own mountain was far from chivalrous so he took his time, bowing to her athletic superiority.

"Here." she said, handing him a pastie, still warm from its perch by the heater.

"I suppose there's no silverware," he said as he opened up the wrapper to the meat and veggie pie wrapped in a golden pie crust.

"Do you think this one time you could eat with your fingers, Johnny?" Jenny said sarcastically.

"You know this could be one of the reasons that folks up here can't move forward."

"John Hendricks," her voice elevating, "I'm having a great time, now, could you just shut up, and eat your pastie!"

"Yes, ma'am."

They finished their lunch and continued down the nine mile long by-pass back to the main high way. With the heavy overcast sky, and the heater on high, Jenny soon fell asleep, and Johnny gave her a nudge as they pulled up in front of her house.

"Hey, I had a great time," she said. "I don't know what your Sunday morning looks like, but if you'd like to escort Helen and I to the 9 a.m. Mass, tomorrow, we'd be honored."

"I'd love to worship with you two, anytime," he said. "I'll firm it up with Helen and see you in the morning."

"Good evening and welcome to Jenny's Jam's on WMTU. I'll be your co-pilot for the next two hours right here in down town Houghton, home of the Michigan Tech Huskies. So kick back, and listen to the sounds of the Motown experience. I'm sending this one out to all of our friends from the Grand Rapids area, hope you're up and listening." Jenny pushed a Temptation CD into the player and called Johnny.

"Are you listening to WMYU radio?" she asked.

"Is Motown still in Detroit?"

"I'm flattered, and I didn't even have to remind you."

"You're the only person I know in Houghton County under the age of sixty. My options are kind of limited."

"Well, I just wanted to tell you I had a great time today. Good night."

Jennifer Parvuu was born with the blond hair and blue eyes that the descendants of Finland are known for, and proud of. The first sixteen years of her life were spent living in an old wood framed two-story house on Caledonia Street in Laurium. Her bedroom on the second floor faced the road, and at night she could see the blinking red lights from the derelict C&H mine, a beacon for airplanes in the area, and little else. She grew up with a miner's mentality, although she'd never been down in one. Across the street were slag heaps of crushed stone left by the mine owners who dug the copper, processed it, poured it into ingots, and sold it to the buyer with the most money. She had been raised to honor the men who went into the hole to feed their families, and helped to create the only life style she ever knew. There was never enough money in the neighborhood to make one family any better than the next. Jenny was happy. Everyone was happy, because everyone knew who they were and that was enough. There were Catholics, Methodists, Lutherans, and folks who just minded their own business. Almost everybody was a descendant of someone from a European country, and tried to bring a little of their heritage to this inhospitable part of northern Michigan.

Jenny knew that she was smart and pretty, and that her future lay somewhere south of Calumet. So, when Michigan Tech offered her a scholarship, she jumped at the chance. She found a room in a home in Hancock with a nice Catholic family and thanked God for the opportunity.

Helen scurried through the living room putting on her earrings.

"Come on Johnny, if we're late we'll end up sitting in the front row and I hate that. You can't see anybody and everybody can see you. Shake a leg. Oh, here comes Jenny up the steps. Come on in Jenny," she called. "We're still waiting for the Missionary to get ready."

"What's all the ruckus about? You'd think the front row was full of Protestants," Johnny said, entering the living room trying to tie his neck tie. "There," Jenny said, adjusting the knot for him. "You'll be the best looking "Troll" in the sanctuary."

"Troll?" he asked.

"People who live below the Big Mac Bridge," Helen said, shooing him out the front door.

"I'm definitely going to say a prayer for both of you this morning if only to improve your senses of humor," he said going down the steps.

They arrived in plenty of time, and Jenny received a lot of smiles as she walked up the steps with a new man on her arm. Johnny nodded at Bob Heikenen, as they took their seats in the back pew. He immediately noticed the dress code was very conservative unlike his younger congregation in Grand Rapids. He was glad he had dressed appropriately so as not to embarrass the ladies. It was his first Catholic Mass and Helen and Jenny on either side of him kept him on his toes, or knees, depending on the situation. Johnny always felt an ecumenical joy that God in His wisdom made everyone different and yet fundamentally the same. After the Mass, Helen and Jenny took him forward to meet Father Walter.

"Good morning, Father," Johnny said. That was a great homily. Your flock is lucky to have you here serving in Hancock."

"Why, thank you," he said, shaking Johnny's hand. "You're John Hendricks. You know, you must be the most famous person in town since, George Gipp; the "Gipper," legendary football player for Notre Dame," the priest said smiling.

"I didn't know he was local," Johnny said.

"Yeah, he has a memorial just north of here in Laurium." Father said.

"Is that anywhere near Tony's pasties?" Johnny asked.

Father looked at Jenny. "Yer teachin dis boy good, eh?"

"I tink so," she said.

"Seriously John, I've heard what you are trying to do and I think we should talk. I'd like to help."

"How about supper at my place, say 6:30 tonight," offered Helen.

"Perfect," said Walter, "What can I bring?"

"Prayers, and ideas," Johnny said. "We can use plenty of both."

"Thank you Jesus!" Johnny said to no one in particular as they drove to Jimmy's restaurant for lunch.

Johnny greeted Father Walter at the front door, hung his coat in the hall closet, and escorted him into the dining room.

"Good evening ladies, I'd appreciate it if you'd all call me Walt, and leave the formalities at the church. I consider Johnny an important addition to our community and I think what we do tonight could have far reaching effects on our youth in Houghton County."

We all took our seats at the oak dinning room table and the good china and cloth napkins let Walt and Johnny know that this was a special occasion.

"Helen, Helen, Helen," Walt fussed. "You always spoil me. John, this is the best cook in Hancock and I am always trying to figure out a way to get myself invited for supper."

"Oh, stop the nonsense before the food gets cold. Johnny will you please bless us with grace?"

> *As they bowed their heads, Johnny could feel the presence of the Lord. "Father, we are blessed to have you with us this evening to share your bounty. We pray not only for the strength your food will provide, but also the strength your Holy Spirit will infuse in us to help the young people of our community. Give us the wisdom and the ability to do your will. Amen."*

"Thank's, Johnny," Helen said. "Jenny will you give me a hand."

After a pleasant dinner, Helen said, "Let's take our tea in the living room; I think it will be more comfortable." Jenny and I sat together on the davenport.

"John," Walt said, "Helen has brought me up to date on what has happened since you arrived, and I must admit I am not surprised at what has happened, or the positions taken. I represent most of the clergy in the area as part of the HHCA, the Houghton Hancock Clergy Association. We meet on the third Tuesday of every month and discuss matters of concern that are relative to all our congregations, and things we can do collectively to show spiritual unity in the community. I have been asked to invite you to Tuesday's meeting, not only to welcome you, but to discuss joining in your cause. What you are proposing has been needed here for a long time. I'm sure that it comes as no surprise that many of our problems come from kids outside the faith, and consequently we have a youth offender, drug and alcohol abuse problem, not to mention abortions and suicides. I'm not saying that church kids are any better than the others, but the rest won't seek help or confide in us. It's really frustrating to lose the ones we don't have a shot at."

"You know, I never considered there would be a resistance from the city once they understood what our purpose was, and I think that is a big part of the problem," Johnny said.

"My folks helped create similar missions in Grand Rapids, for inner city kids, and once the boys and girls saw that it was their club, they all started coming. I'm not saying it's a perfect situation, but it helps a lot of kids with no place to go, or no one to turn to. We even developed a better relationship with the police and welfare organizations. They were both instrumental in helping us put a lot of good families back together."

Johnny took a sip of his lukewarm tea, and set it back on the coffee table.

"I've been mulling this over since yesterday," he said, "and I think the best plan is to write an editorial tomorrow in the Mining Gazette explaining to the citizens in the area what we are trying to do. It would be a simple straight forward story of where I come from, what qualifies me to open a youth mission, and why it would be successful in Hancock. If the under-represented people in the area think that it might be useful in their lives, maybe they'll show up Wednesday night, just out of curiosity."

"I think that's a great idea," said Walt. Usually the editorial page is full of complaints and negative positions, and this certainly will liven up the Council Meeting. I think we'll get a fair shake from Bob Heikenen, and your landlady here holds a lot of sway among the long-time residents in town. I'll shake the bushes with the local clergy tomorrow and see if we can pack the Hall with citizens who care more about their young people than they do about a dusty old building."

"Here, here," said Helen as she jumped up to refill the tea cups. "With great minds like yours and Johnny's, I think the future of Hancock looks brighter, don't you Jenny? See if you can find that plate of macaroons I left on the kitchen table, dear."

After working out some of the details of their plans, which included Jenny's position at MTU, as well as the radio station, everyone agreed to touch base on Monday. We all stood as Father Walter offered up a prayer of hope and said good-night.

CHAPTER 5

"I'm sorry Mr. Hendricks, but we need to have at least one more day to meet deadline. If we had this editorial on Saturday maybe, but today no way. However, I must admit we do need more eye openers like this in our newspaper. Yes indeed," said the frizzy-haired, bespectacled young girl with a pencil stuck behind her ear, standing behind the counter at the Mining Gazette. "Hey, I've got a better idea," she exploded. "Why don't we have one of our beat writers interview you right now, along with a couple of pictures," she said marveling at her bright idea.

Johnny was trying to understand this exuberant scattershot approach to conversation, but wasn't having much luck. "Uh, okay, if you think that's possible."

"Ronnie," the girl shouted down the hall, "grab Gino and meet me in the second interview room ASAP. By the way, John, I can call you John can't I?"

"Uh, sure."

"Anyway, my name is Wanda, and I'm sick and tired of those narrow minded old poops in Hancock standing in the way of progress. If you can help one kid …"

"Wanda?" Johnny asked.

"Ronnie, get in here," she spat.

"What," shouted a stodgy fortyish man with thinning hair rushing down the hall.

"Ronnie, this is Mr. Hendricks, the gentleman who is opening the Youth Mission in Hancock. You need to interview him for tomorrow's edition. Now, go get Gino and his camera."

Two minutes later, all was ready.

"When did you know you wanted to open a mission?" asked Ronnie, hitting the record button on his pocket recorder.

"That's a good question, and I'm not sure I have a good answer. I think I've always known what I wanted to do. I mean, I never wanted to be the leader, or star of the team. Money or power was never high on my list, or even popularity. No, the only thing that has consistently given me that inner joy is to be the person behind the person." Johnny paused. "Being a preacher's kid hasn't always been easy, but being secure in myself and my faith has made me a lightning rod for those who were going through a bad time. I am blessed to have strong parents who have lived their lives by principles drawing their strength from each other and ultimately from God. There is a great comfort in knowing that while the rest of the world around you is searching for answers, I know Whose I am," Johnny said with confidence.

"Are you telling me this is going to be a church mission?" Ronnie asked, sensing a chink in Johnny's armor.

"A church mission? No, I think we should call it a world mission. It's not necessary to have a specific sponsor, or be represented by a particular faith, or denomination. There are no restrictions on kindness or generosity. There is no one who should be denied the opportunity to share what was given to all of us. I look forward to meeting all of the youth in our area. We all have needs, and we all have something to offer. Being a teenager is one of the most difficult periods in a person's life. Many of the decisions that they make, or don't make can greatly affect their futures. Sometimes a chat with a friend or a peer can give them the insight into something that has been troubling them for a long time. I don't want to save anybody. I just want to open a clean and wholesome facility where kids can come in and get away from the pressures of life."

"Well then, why the big fuss?" Ronnie asked as Gino rushed into the room holding his light meter towards Johnny's face.

"That's another good question, but perhaps, a better one would be, where's the good? If a youth mission would harm the city of Hancock, than who would it harm? Would it bring blight to the city center or alter the façade of the Aho Building in this beautiful historical district. The answer is no. A good cleaning and more activity would only enhance the charm of the whole area."

Gino was flitting around the room shooting close-ups, and sensing something big was happening right here in front of him.

"Would it bring people you don't know into the downtown community?" Johnny posed the question. "Hopefully, by its very nature, it is designed to bring all kinds of youths together to meet, talk, and find common ground in a positive supervised environment. You could call it a teen United Nations Organization right here in your own neighborhood. In our county we don't restrict people that are different from coming to our schools. That's what makes us stronger. Hancock hosts a great Finnish American Festival every year for this very purpose. What if the first immigrants from Helsinki had been prevented from living here because they were different? What if the Cornish miners from England were sent back? We would never have eaten a pastie. If you are a proud member of this community whose ancestors didn't come from any place in particular, but would love to see us thrive and grow through the strength of our youth, as well as the wisdom of our community leaders, come to the Council Meeting on Wednesday night at 7:30. I would love to meet you and hear your ideas."

"Bravo," shouted Wanda standing in the hallway surrounded by most of the staff.

Johnny shook everyone's hand and thanked them for their support. As he walked down Sheldon Street to his van, he could feel his life starting to change.

"I feel like a politician running for office," he told Jenny on the phone. "They promised to have it in tomorrow's paper, a full day ahead of the meeting. I'm going to call mom, and give her the news. I'll call you later, Bye."

'It's Johnny," Angie shouted, putting Johnny on speaker.

"Hi, son," said dad.

"I'm glad I caught you both at home, I've got great news."

Johnny told them both about the coming newspaper story, and his collaboration with the HHCA to jointly support the mission.

"Johnny we prayed for your success in both of our churches yesterday, and the response at the coffee hour after the service was gratifying. So many people offered to help through prayer and financial gifts, that we were overwhelmed," dad said.

"And the hand of the Holy Spirit has brought us all together to do His good works." Angie said. "We are so happy for you, Johnny. Can you rent us a couple of rooms at the Hancock Motel for Wednesday night?"

"I'd love to; I've got some good folks I want you to meet."

"Brothers and sisters, I'd like you to meet a new friend of ours, Johnny Hendricks." Father Walter said, as he entered the Fellowship Hall in the First Methodist Church of Hancock. A group of clergy broke up from their small chat groups and surrounded him with smiles, making Johnny feel like the Prodigal Son. After shaking hands, and exchanging pleasantries, Father Walter asked everyone to take seats at the big round table to begin the meeting.

"Johnny, I took advantage of connections I have at the Mining Gazette, and secured ten copies of today's newspaper before it went to general distribution," Father Walter said, "I believe the term is "hot off the press." He smiled as he passed them around the table. "Take a minute to read the feature interview on page four. It will give you an idea of what our special guest has in store for our fair city."

The preachers quickly found the interview, admired the photos, and delved right into the story. There was silence as everyone read about the most exciting thing to happen in Houghton County, in some time.

"Oh, they're not going to like this," said Thelma Jenkins, Pastor of the Grace United Methodist Church in Houghton.

"It's a real kick in the pants," added Captain Jim Mueller of the Salvation Army Community Church down by the river on Ravine Street.

Father Walter just grinned at the effect the newspaper time bomb had on the local clergy, and added. "In a few hours, everyone in Houghton-Hancock will know John

Hendricks, and what his vision is. Those of us, who have lived in the community for a while, are aware of what some of the council members will hurl at him to try and crush any hope of a youth mission. It would be foolish to think that even half of our parishioners will embrace such a novel idea. Let's face it folks, nobody likes change, especially when it comes to our downtown area."

"It's about time somebody stood up and did something!" vented Mel Simpson from the Community Presbyterian Church on the hill in Houghton. "The historical area is decaying right before our eyes, and no one seems to care. I think John is a God-send, and we need to use our pulpits to help spread the word."

Everyone nodded in agreement as Johnny squirmed in his chair.

Rising slowly, he said, "I am very grateful to God that you share what I would like to do here, but we have to understand that half a loaf is not enough. If we put the city council on the defensive, we will divide the citizens of this area, and that is not our mission. These are not evil men or women in the City Council. In fact, they are probably the most dedicated people in the city. They weren't elected because they were different, they were chosen because they were like us in many ways. I did that interview yesterday to bring awareness to what we could do if we work together. I don't want to challenge them. I want to co-operate with them. I want to make them an "us".

The flock sat quietly as Johnny sat down. He reached his hands out in each direction and in joining hands he said, Father, please remove the contention from our hearts, and fill them with loving gratitude for the opportunity before us. Help us to listen tomorrow night, as well as to speak, so that good people can work together in harmony for a place that will benefit our youths to live better and more productive lives. Amen

Father Walter threw his arm around John, hugged him and said, "You ought to be a preacher," and everybody laughed.

The rest of the afternoon, Johnny walked along the path along Portage Lake enjoying the warm breezes and the afternoon sun. Why was it always man against man; my idea versus your idea. *Lord, why is there always confrontation?* He silently prayed. *I'm sorry I acted like such a fool in City Hall, but wasn't it Your plan to use me to help You build a mission in Hancock?*

Father, I've made such a mess of things, please forgive me for not putting You first in everything I do. Guide me in the meeting tomorrow night, so that Your presence will be felt and Your Will will be done. Thank you for allowing me to be Your servant. Amen

Johnny sat on a bench chucking stones in the water, feeling a growing confidence.

CHAPTER 6

Kitty spent most of Tuesday full of self pity and went to work having done nothing to help R.J. He would just have to wait. On Wednesday morning she got up early and prepared for battle. Upon entering the police station she got the bad news. The police had taken the three boys down to Escanaba an hour before she got to the lock-up. The smirks on the officers' faces as she walked out the door were more than she could take. "What do they think I'm supposed to do?" She asked the rearview mirror as she started driving south to find her son. "I'm going to miss a day's pay. Jimmy's running around doing God knows what. I've got no money and nobody to help me." Kitty pounded the wheel and swerved off the road, killed the engine, flopped down across the seat and burst into tears. *What am I supposed to do God?* She thought. *Do you think I wanted it to turn out like this? I can't stand it anymore. What can I say or do that will make a difference in R.J.'s life? He's got it made. He wouldn't trade places with me for all the money in the world, and I don't blame him. What can I possibly say to him that will make any difference?*

God, he'll just look at me with that stupid look on his face. It's hopeless.

Kitty sat up, blew her nose into a wadded up tissue, started the car and made a U-turn. There was no point in driving all that way and wasting all that gas, she reasoned. *I'll go back to Maggie's house and maybe she'll buy me lunch.*

"How you doing Sis?" Maggie said as Kitty entered the house dangling the car keys.

"You tell me what I can do," Kitty said accusingly to her older sister. "I don't have an important husband who runs the city. I don't have a fancy house overlooking the lake. You've got it all. I've got nothing," she vented as she flopped down on the couch in a world of self pity.

Maggie had heard it all before. Katherine, as their mother had called her, was the darling of the family growing up. Margaret, being five years older, was the baby sitter and from the age of ten was responsible for keeping her little sister out of trouble. Mother, not mom, had a position in the community, and chose adult relationships in place of family life. Dad was afraid of Mother, so their stations in life were pretty well established. Love was not an emotion that was displayed by the parents, and Margaret was quick to learn the rules. The warmth and closeness that Katherine needed was unavailable, so the baby of the family became a tyrant like her mother.

Katherine became Kitty in 9ᵗʰ grade, when unknown hormones and social pressures exploded in the worst ways. Kitty became an outlaw. Stories were circulated about her around the high school, which weren't true, but the added attention she got from the boys eased her loneliness. Authority and discipline merely emboldened her until she was expelled from the Hancock School System, and she couldn't have been happier. She had just turned sixteen and was ready to take on the world, but the world in Hancock wasn't ready for her. It was easier to consider her an incorrigible and cast her aside than to try and find some redeeming value in her. Kitty rose early every morning, got dressed, and hit the streets. She'd walk across the bridge into Houghton and found other young people hanging out in the park near the MTU campus. This group of college under classmen, and high school dropouts were experiencing a new found freedom with unlimited responsibility and marginal supervision. This gave Kitty a false sense of camaraderie. Life was a fantasy to her and most of the kids she met hated the system and parental control. She hung out with every sort of dreamer and idler a college campus could provide. It was always exciting, but never compensated for the emptiness she felt walking back across the bridge to her home where she wasn't welcome. Then she met Robert.

To understand Robert you first had to understand where he came from, and you might as well start with Little Harold, Robert's dad.

Harold Hackala literally crawled out from behind a copper stamp sand mound and took his place along side the rest of the young men and women trying to make a fresh start in a time called the post war era. Because of his height and bad feet, he managed to miss the draft and spent the war hunting and fishing and very little else.

Being poor wasn't a crime in those days, and the people on the Keweenaw got used to it. Most of the copper mining had collapsed years ago, and a lot of old timers sat in the local bars, drank beer, and cursed the Calumet Heckla Mining Company. The jobs had all gone to South America or out west, and the only thing that remained was the bitterness. It was a feeling that was easy to explain, and easy to understand, but hard to live with.

"Pull it a little tighter," Uno Svenbladt said to Little Harold who helped take the play out of the single strand wire. The ruse of unknown origin was once again being performed. This time by the two deer slayers who were determined to drive a herd of white tail deer between two Ironwood trees with the thin strand of wire stretched in the middle to snap their necks. The out come was obvious, but the ability to frighten the deer at the precise moment so that they would panic and stampede down the trail to certain death was what gave these nefarious poachers bragging rights down at Shute's Bar in Calumet. And brag they did, accepting free beers along with the occasional shot of Kessler's whiskey.

"You could hear em comin from way down in da swamp," Little Harold said, lifting his red and black hunting cap to scratch a head that hadn't seen soap and water for a while.

"There musta been a dozen of em," Uno overstated. "But after the first seven went down, the rest of em got smart and ran back down to da swamp."

There was a general agreement among the band of hunting denizens that this was acceptable behavior for the deer and the hunters, and a great deal of shouting and bottle clinking ensued. In the rugged wilderness of the U.P. the question of right and wrong, fair and unfair, or good and evil seemed to change from generation to generation depending on the needs of the people who were trying to survive.

Robert John was born in the Laurium Memorial Hospital on a night in February when the likes of Jack London, the legendary north woods novelist, would have stayed home. One hundred and forty inches of snow had already fallen on the Keweenaw since winter began in early November, and the gales blowing off of Lake Superior had a way of distributing snow like gravy on mashed potatoes.

Actually, Harold and Alma, Robert's mom and dad, were forced to walk the three blocks to the hospital wrapped in heavy quilts, because all the snow plows were out on the highway between Calumet and Copper Harbor. What made the situation even more absurd was that no one even mentioned the weather when they entered the dry and warm lobby. And while the storm was raging out side, baby Robert did the same in the arms of his mother.

While Harold taught Robert everything he could about hunting and trapping, his son was drawn to the lakes. As a young boy, Robert would drive his dad's old truck all over the peninsula fishing Lake Medora for walleye; Bete Grise for salmon, and Slaughter Lake for the biggest pike in the county. He was known as a master angler, and a sportsman, but as he grew older, the need to put gas in his truck and food on the table drove him into poaching. The Indian population had been taking fish illegally for a long time as one of the conditions of some old treaty. Robert decided if they could do it so could he, and he was good at it.

The politicians in Lansing had no idea what life on the Keweenaw was like. Most had never even been to the U.P. and now they wanted to tell him how to live. They may have stopped his dad from harvesting venison to sell to the locals, but there was no way they were going to stop him from doing what he did best.

✹

—————

CHAPTER 7

"Hey didn't I see you walkin across da bridge yesterday," a rough greasy haired young man smelling like raw fish said, sliding onto a stool next to Kitty. Kaleva's was filling up fast and there wasn't another seat available for her to move to.

Kitty thought, I may be down on my luck, but I'm not this far down.

"I'll have the number 2, with bacon," he told the waitress, as she set down some silverware. He leaned over towards Kitty, "Shouldn't you be in school?"

"Not that it's any of your business, but I don't go there anymore." She spat back.

"Too smart for em, eh," he said with kind of a knowing grin, as the waitress filled his coffee cup. "I was too smart for em too." When the two over easy with hash browns and bacon arrived, he said, "My names Robert Hackala. What's yours?"

"Kitty," she said, "Don't you work?"

"I don't work, I'm a fisherman." He responded, with a mouth full of eggs.

"Are you rich?" She asked sarcastically looking at his ragged attire.

"No, but I make good money selling perch and lake trout at the back doors of the local restaurants. I've got five nice lake trout iced up in the back of my truck ready to deliver right after breakfast, you want to come along?" Robert drenched his potatoes in ketchup.

"No, I'm kind of busy."

"Suit yourself," he said. "I'm going to Copper Harbor. It might be kind of fun."

"You probably don't have room in your truck," her voice hesitated.

"Sup to you," Robert finished his coffee and paid his bill. He went to the men's room, and when he went outside, Kitty was leaning on his front fender.

"When will we be back?" she asked indifferently.

"We'll see," he said as they climbed in the truck.

It started out as a relationship between two outcasts. They both had chips on their shoulders and that drew them closer together. Robert knew she was much younger than he was, so it became sort of a show off, hero worship relationship, and that was fine with both of them. Kitty had never experienced the great outdoors, and Robert was more than happy to show it to her. She learned to set the hook in the mouth of a huge lake trout in Lake Superior, and wrestle it into the boat like a real sportsman. She could fish the bayous of Lac La Belle, and bring in jumbo yellow-bellied perch three at a time on their special rigs. It became more important to please Robert than anything else in her life. He became her life. Late at night, lying on the hood of his old pick-up truck, watching shooting stars high above Bete Grise, they would talk about their dreams and what their future might bring. They began to act alike, dress alike, and even think alike. It was the happiest time in both of their lives. Her parents suspected she had found someone, but frankly didn't care. Although they were closer than many married couples, they maintained their platonic relationship. It was important that they didn't mess this thing up. They had no where else to go.

Two years later, they had grown together, and became very successful in the wholesale fish industry. They rented a shabby two story house in Laurium, and her parents said good riddance. Kitty wanted to get married, and Robert didn't care one way or another. She talked to the Chaplin at MTU and a wedding picnic was planned for the following Saturday at Haven Falls Park on the shores of Lac La Belle. No family was invited; no family came. A few fishermen, some neighbors, and a couple of friends surrounded the happy couple as the Chaplin performed the ceremony by the waterfalls. As a battery operated cassette recorder played "Chrystal Blue Persuasion" by Tommy James and the Shondells, they tied the knot beneath the over-hanging boughs of the towering Michigan white pines. After the festivities the happy couple drove to Marquette for dinner at the Ponderosa and their honeymoon night at the Motel 6.

It was a marriage that was doomed from the start. It was never a loving relationship, because neither had ever seen or experienced love in their lives. Robert continued to be the boss, and Kitty the employee. It wasn't bad, but it wasn't good. In fact, it was just kind of disappointing, and that was the problem. Neither knew how to fix it. They heard all the songs, and saw all the movies, but nothing in the lives of a couple of lake trout fishermen seemed to generate that warm feeling they had expected. Soon, Kitty was expecting, and couldn't fish. Then, Robert started stopping at the bar at night, and the next dozen years rolled by like a bad soap opera. Their first born son, R.J., named after his dad, was slow. He wasn't like the other kids; He just sat in his play pen and stared at her. Robert took him everywhere, but they always left her home alone. It seemed like she didn't fit in anywhere, anymore. Robert's mother, Alma, would take R.J. to give Kitty and Robert time alone, but he was always too busy fixing equipment or buying something. He called her a nag, but she honestly didn't know what to do with herself, then, when she became pregnant with Jimmie, Robert leased a barn, did all his boat fixing there, and never came home. The night Jimmie was born; Grandpa Harold looked all over Laurium for Robert, but never did find him.

Three gongs on the ship's clock above the television in Maggie's living room woke up Kitty from a sound sleep. It took a moment to figure out where she was, and what her circumstances were, but as her mind began to focus the memory of her fight with her sister all came back to her. As she sat up, she listened for any sound in the house, but it was deathly quiet. Maggie must have gone out. Good riddance. She was never on her side anyway. Nobody was. Kitty smiled to herself and thought, maybe I'll walk down to the bar and treat myself to one of those hot steak sandwiches and a couple of beers. This town can't keep old Kitty down.

Kitty pulled her hat down over her ears as she left the house in Terrace Park, and walked down the hill towards the center of Hancock. Even the rush of the swirling leaves blowing in every direction couldn't dampen her mood.

"Hi Kitty," Rudy hollered, as she blew through the front door of Rudy's bar. "What are you doing here? I thought you were going to Escanaba."

"Ah, things got fouled up. You know how that goes, so I thought I'd stop in and let you make me one of your special steak sandwiches with lots of fried onions on it."

"Hey, I know how you like em kid. Here, take your coat off and let me pour you a beer, you look like you had a rough day."

Kitty reached over the bar and grabbed today's copy of the Mining Gazette. Glancing through the front section, she saw the picture of Johnny, and began to read the interview. After reading half the article, she said, "You know Rudy, here's a guy who seems to have it all together. I mean, he comes to town, doesn't even know a soul, but knows there are some messed up kids here and he wants to help em, eh. Go and figure."

"Speaking of kids, who's watching Jimmy?" Rudy asked.

Kitty dropped the paper, staring at the face in the mirror behind the bar, trying to remember the last time she had seen her youngest son's face. Rudy stood and watched as she slid from the barstool and slowly backed out the door.

"Kitty, your coat, your purse," Rudy shouted racing for the door.

Kitty stopped, but not to retrieve her possessions. She truly had no idea which way to go. Jimmy wasn't home last night; he wasn't home this morning, and he probably wasn't home now. Zipping up her coat, she numbly climbed the hill to her apartment with tears running down her face. She ran through the unlocked side door calling out his name, but found the place just as she had left it earlier in the day. If Jimmy had left before or after she had gone to borrow the car, she didn't know. She did know he was going to get it when she found him, of that she was sure.

Jimmy's first memory of being on earth was of being cold. It seemed like he was always cold. Winter in Laurium could be brutal. Mama would put R.J. and him on the sled and drag them up the hill along the snow covered sidewalk into downtown Laurium to the used clothing store. Dad's only work in the winter-time was to drag the deep snow off the roof tops of houses for a few dollars to help make ends meet, but there wasn't much left for clothing. It seemed like little Jimmy was always sick and it was always snowing. Even at an early age, R.J. would collect newspapers from the neighbors to stuff in the rafters of their upstairs bedroom to help keep out the winter wind. The boys would sleep together and Kitty would cover them with lots of old quilts donated by Harold and Alma. There were so many in fact that they couldn't roll over. They didn't complain about the rough conditions because everyone in the U.P. was experiencing the same thing. As they grew older, it was always R.J. and Jimmy together. Wherever they went, it was always R.J. the leader, Jimmy the follower. R.J. didn't like it, but it was his job. With Robert spending more and more time away from home, and Kitty relieved of her motherly responsibilities, both parents began to look for outside interests. R.J. didn't care; it was easier than listening to them fight all the time. The balloon burst when Robert came home drunk one night and began pushing Kitty around. R.J. got between the two adults, and paid for it with a black eye. Kitty threatened to call the police. Robert said something he couldn't take back and stomped out the door.

"When you get done hangin dem cables, put dem batteries on dat pallet." Victor shouted at Jimmy, as he spat yellow tobacco juice out of the side of his gray bearded mouth. This was either a blessing or a curse, he thought, and he hadn't decided which, but to have R.J.'s kid brother fall into his lap like this was certainly unexpected to say the least. Victor Wurtz didn't get many visitors on his property in the scrub lands out west of Baraga, and he liked it that way. He had inherited these forty acres, and it provided good cover for his junkyard, and towing business. There were certainly plenty of wrecked cars in the Houghton-Hancock area, and when Victor had towed enough of these junkers to his crusher, he could haul them all down to Marquette for a big profit. Actually, the wrecks just paid the rent. The real fat came from the stolen car parts that R.J. and some of his friends in the area pilfered from the unsuspecting citizens in the nearby towns. Victor didn't consider himself a criminal, merely an opportunist. He had spent his whole life trying to adapt to his neighbors lifestyles, but he was never accepted by them. He lived a solitary life under the radar, as they say, with no one the wiser. That was until Monday when R.J. and his buddy's got caught boosting a new battery and ended up in the clink. R.J. had called him to go up to Hancock and pick up his kid brother Jimmy and bring him back to the junkyard in Baraga. At least Jimmy would be safe, and the welfare people wouldn't take him away. Only R.J. and Victor knew where Jimmy was and that was good. Who knows how long he'd be locked up? Brothers had to look out for each other.

A day never went by when Victor didn't think about that horrible night fifty years ago. Waking up his younger brother Klaus, and seeing the flames. He could still hear the screams of "Dirty Nazis" as the town's people of L'Anse burned their house and barn to the ground. The horse and cows were chased into the night, and the Wurtz family was lucky to escape with their lives. They lost everything but the little savings they had hidden. All of the German-American farms in the township were burned that night as the hate for Hitler spread across the country. American boys were dying and there was no other way to help the cause. The Wurtz family drove by the light of the house fires to Skanee town at the end of the peninsula to stay with relatives that night, and Victor never forgot it. There was no room for them to stay, so the next morning, the family moved south through the Huron Mountains, and Victor, being the oldest, was farmed out to Ralph Aitima, a friend of his dads.

Ralph was a collector plain and simple. If you didn't want it, or it wasn't nailed down, it went into the back of Ralph's old 38 Ford stake truck. Ralph and Eileen were childless, so Vic, as they called him became an Aitima. He was welcomed, loved, and much appreciated, and an extra pair of hands made life easier for everyone. Fish and game were plentiful, and Eileen had a small vegetable garden.

Plus, Ralph used to joke, things in the scrap business were always picking up. Vic accepted his new life and was a quick learner, and figured out how to bargain in scrap to his advantage without any trouble. However, when Vic went to bed at night, he knew he would always be Victor Wurtz. He never forgot where he came from or how he got there, and he never saw his family again.

A strange phenomenon occurred ten years after World War Two. The old timers, called it insanity, but the youngsters called it rock and roll. And in no time those old rust buckets sitting out in farmers fields became hot-rods, and there was Ralph and his family ready to join the revolution. Overnight, the need for classic car chassis', fenders, and hoods, not to mention bumpers and tail lights had gone out of sight, and there was the Aitima Junk Yard to fill the demand.

Ralph and Eileen died within a month of each other in the early 1960's and left everything to Vic. In the twenty years he had lived with the Aitimas, he had truly become their son, and had learned many lessons from the way they lived. They had taught him loyalty and respect for each other, frugality, and most of all, lend a hand to a friend in need. He buried them together in a little Finnish cemetery in Pelkie by Otter Lake. Ralph never trusted banks and had always hidden his wealth on the family property beneath a big stone by a giant white pine tree. When he explained that most of his money had never been seen by the Tax Man, and what was there was none of the government's business, Vic understood. With forty acres, a substantial cash reserve, and a growing scrap and car parts business, Vic was a wealthy man. The first thing he did was to legally change his name back to Victor Wurtz. The second thing he did was to hang a large metal sign across the entrance of the property announcing

VICTOR WURTZ'S SCRAP
AND USED CAR PARTS

He erected a chain link fence around the scrap area of the business with a padlocked gate in the front. People driving by wondered why anyone would want to lock up junk. Victor sat in the little work shed in the middle of his property and smiled.

Another part of the counter-culture phenomenon was the desire to tune in, turn on and drop out. Victor never really understood the tune in, turn on part, but when the teenagers in the Keweenaw began to drop out, he was there to catch them. When he was a teen he never had a chance to drop out, but he sure knew what it was like to be young and alone.

CHAPTER 8

The wind was raw out of the north with a rough chop off the breakwater as Johnny, Helen, and Jenny sat in the Lobby of the Hancock Motel watching the parking lot through the misted front window. Johnny's folks and Grandpa had left Grand Rapids at 6 am, and with no delays were expected any time. Johnny sat nervously bouncing his leg and checking the clock behind the registration counter.

"You know, there are a thousand places I'd rather be right now, and I don't know why," he said to Helen. "I mean, I know we're doing the right thing, and everything seems to be going our way, but," Johnny hesitated. "It's just the first time I've been out in front. Do you know what I mean? Why couldn't I start at the bottom like everybody else? Why couldn't I have somebody tell me what to do, and simply do it? Helen, I'm getting a little scared."

"You mean like David and Goliath, or Daniel in the lion's den," Helen replied.

Johnny got up and walked over to the water cooler for a drink.

"I think it's them," Jenny said, as a late model Lincoln Town Car pulled up under the entrance.

The trunk popped open as three weary travelers slowly escaped from the luxury vehicle after much too long a ride.

"Hi, Mom" Johnny said as he helped his mother from the rear seat. Dad and Grandpa slowly crawled out, stretched, and slowly made their way over toward Johnny.

"They couldn't have put this place any farther away, could they?" Grandpa joked as he threw his arms around his grandson.

Helen and Jenny were introduced to the family and after hugs and hand shakes, the five made their way into the warm lobby while Johnny parked the car. While the folks registered, Johnny and Jenny took care of the luggage.

"I made reservations for dinner here in the Motel, then you can rest up, and we can discuss the presentation."

"That sounds great," said dad, "I'm starved."

"Howard I tell you she was out of her mind." Maggie said, "And after everything we've done for her, she attacked me right in my own living room, and then passed out like a common drunk."

"Look Maggie, I don't want to hear about it. I've got a lot of things on my mind tonight." Howard said. "There's a very important meeting at 7:30 and I know that Heikinen is going to try and pull a fast one on me. If that young "do gooder" from down state shows up and thinks he can come in here and throw a little money around, and take over our city, he doesn't know Howard Berg. We don't need any outsider trying to tell us how to take care of our young people. We've been raising our kids as long as anybody else, and haven't had any complaints. The very idea infuriates me."

"Calm down Howard, you know what happens to your stomach when you get aggravated. You'd better go upstairs and take one of your pills and lie down for a little while."

"The last thing I need is to lie down. I need to show these people that they can't take over our town. Period."

Howard walked over to the telephone and called three of his supporters and once again explained to them the importance of being on time and supporting his position. He finally sat down to supper realizing he had done everything he could do, but his stomach was still rolling.

"Hancock Police Department, Officer Meaden speaking."

"This is Kitty Hackala, I'd like to report a missing person."

The afternoon mist had turned into a steady sleet by 6:00 and the county trucks were out sanding the roads in preparation for a slippery night. The City Hall external lights were on, and the sidewalks in front were salted in preparation for the council meeting. All members were required to be present for the 6:30 work session, which always preceded the regular meeting to review the agenda items. By 6:15, all of the principals were in the hall. There was more tension than usual as Howard Berg had sequestered his group of followers in one of the side rooms for a private meeting. Bob Heikinen, and the other three council members sat in their usual chairs and discussed the weather. A few minutes later Howard led his flock into council chambers.

"Great weather for ducks," Bob joked casually to no one in particular, but the Berg contingency sat quietly sensing amiability a sign of weakness. The Hancock City Council was silent until 6:30 when Bob Heikinen gaveled the work meeting to order.

"I see that we're all present, I guess we can begin with any carry over business from last month." Bob said, nodding to Bertha Mittila, the clerk of session.

"Nothing from last month, Bob," said Bertha.

"New business," asked Bob.

"A young man from Grand Rapids named John Hendricks has asked to address the council for permission to ask for a work permit to open the old Aho Building on Quincy Street for the purpose of renovating and opening a youth mission for the young people of Houghton County," Bertha said.

"Are there any preliminary thoughts on the subject?" Bob queried.

Howard began to rise, pushing back his chair, and clearing his throat at the same time.

"Mr. Heikinen," he said much too formally, "I would like to make a motion to take a vote right here and now to prevent this young man from presenting this program to the council tonight, or any other night. I say," as his voice elevated, "for the protection of the city's historical district and our local youth, we the fathers, and public representatives have a responsibility to do what's best for the City of Hancock as well as the surrounding area."

With a certain amount of bluster and nodding to his supporters, Howard took his seat.

"Would somebody like to second that?" Bob asked.

"Second," said Tim Murphy, one of Howard's loyalists.

"Well, before we take a vote, I think it's only fair to have a preliminary discussion. Does anyone think that's unfair?" Bob asked hoping someone would raise their hand.

The room was silent except for the wind whistling outside the window.

"I've got a question for you, Howard. Have you ever met this John Hendricks?" Bob asked rocking back in his chair with his hands folded across his stomach.

"Well, no, but I've heard plenty about him from enough people to know that he's one of those young religious radicals who goes into towns and starts trouble between parents and their children. We've never had that in this town before, and we don't need it now. I'm not saying that there aren't places around the world where a man like that couldn't do some good, but not here in our town."

"I've met the young man," said Bob calmly. "I've talked to his dad, and they're both fine Christian men. Young John, Johnny, as everyone calls him, has endeared himself to a number of fine people in our community. He has the support of the local clergy association, the news paper, and a lot of young folks. I won't say that he's right; I just say that he's come too far not to get a chance to be heard. Are we ready for a vote?"

All eight members nodded yes.

"Bob should we record this, or just a show of hands?" Bertha asked.

"Just a show of hands," Howard grumbled.

"All of you, who would like to hear Johnny speak, raise your hand." Bob said.

All of Bob's side plus one of Howard's and Bertha raised their hand."

"I'm sorry, Bertha," Bob said, "but I'm afraid you're not aloud to vote on this one, but I admire your spirit."

Howard and his two remaining followers jumped up in a huff and headed for the exit. The door burst open and the hallway was a crush of people trying to get seats for the meeting, pushing Howard and his minions back into the chamber.

Tom Burley, the Hancock Chief of Police, pushed his way through the mayhem to Bob Heikenen's microphone, and shouted for silence. It took a few seconds for the pandemonium to subside.

"I have an announcement to make," he shouted. "I am the Chief of Police. We have a missing child in the community." Suddenly all of the air was sucked out of the building. "Now listen. Now is not the time to panic. The child's name is James, Jimmy Hackala. He is the son of Kitty Hackala, and the nephew of Howard Berg, one of our councilmen. We know he's been gone since at least early this morning, and we don't know anything else. The council meeting has been postponed, and will be rescheduled. The Hancock, Houghton, county and State Police agencies have all been alerted and we will pass on information as it becomes available. If you have any knowledge of where Jimmy might be, please call us now. It's cold out there. Thank you."

The stunned group made their way down the stairs to the street as the fierce wind and sleet blasted their faces. Everyone wondered what had happened to the poor little boy, and prayed that he wasn't out in this terrible weather.

CHAPTER 9

"Mrs. Hackala, we've found your ex-husband in Laurium, and the state police are driving him down here to Hancock to help in the investigation." Detective Tom Martin said.

The two sisters sat huddled on the broken-down couch as Maggie held Kitty's hand. The police had been coming and going, and talking to the neighbors, but so far no one had any ideas as to where Jimmy could be. Kitty told Martin that her son R.J. knew more about Jimmy than anyone, but the police had him locked up in prison down in Escanaba, and she had no way of getting a hold of him. Maggie took the Detective into the kitchen and explained that R.J. had just been put into youth detention, and a couple of phone calls were made. So far, nobody knew anything. The front door blew open as a blast of cold air filled the living room. Two state troopers followed by Robert, with that, "I told you so" look on his face directed at Kitty, entered the room. He was dressed in his camouflage and hunters orange jacket, and a two week growth of beard. You could tell by the smell of cigarette smoke, and stale beer where they had found him. The cold from outside was no worse than the stares between Jimmy's parents.

"You must be Robert, Jimmy's dad," Tom Martin reached to shake his hand. "Why don't you sit next to Mrs. Hackala on the couch, and let's see if we can figure out where Jimmy is and get him home tonight."

Kitty burst into angry tears and reached over and slammed Robert in the side of his face with a tight fist. "As if you ever cared about any of us," she howled. "All you care about is your beer, cigarettes, and women. We always came last. Yer da problem. Yer da reason somebody's got my little boy. If anything happens to Jimmy, yer goin to jail. I'll see to dat."

Robert jumped up and started to leave, but one of the troopers grabbed him by the arm, and detained him.

"Kitty, Robert, this isn't helping us find Jimmy," Martin said. "Robert sit over there by the table, please."

Robert flopped down into a straight backed chair and stared at the floor.

"Now, here's what we know," said Martin, trying to regain control. "We talked to Ms. Merkle, Jimmy's teacher. She says he hasn't been in class for a week. He skips school most of the time, and even when he comes to class, he just stares out the window. She says she has made appointments to talk with you Kitty, but you never respond, so she stopped trying."

"Hey, I'm sorry, I gotta work too. You folks think its easy workin full time and raising two teenage boys, I ..."

"Excuse me Kitty," Tom interrupted, "We're not here to place blame. We're here to figure out where Jimmy spends most of his time when he's supposed to be in school. Now, there must be somebody who has seen him or spends time with him who can help us find him. Kitty, who are his friends? Who does he walk home from school with? There must be somebody he talks to you about that can tell us anything about this young man's life."

Kitty stared at the wall, while everyone stared at Kitty.

Martin rose from the chair saying, "We will continue working leads and searching through the night to find Jimmy. I am assigning Officer Shirley Koski to watch your place.

If Jimmy shows up or if you need anything, she is here to help you. Good night."

The men all walked out the front door single file, dropping the temperature in the house 20 degrees.

"If you don't mind, Sis, I'll spend the night," offered Maggie.

Kitty scratched her arm.

"Good Morning," Johnny said as he made his way around the breakfast table in the Hancock Motel dining room, offering up hugs and kisses to mom, dad, and grandpa. "any news about the missing little boy from last night?"

"I called the police this morning, and they said nothing yet," said dad.

"Good morning, everybody," Jenny said entering the dining room."

"Jenny's an employee here as well as a full time student at MTU," said Johnny.

"Not to mention a disc jockey extraordinaire on the college radio station," she joked.

"What a gal." Johnny said."

"What a gal, indeed," Mom chimed in. "How do you find time for this guy?"

"It's getting tougher every day," Jenny smiled. "Do you mind if I join you?"

"Our pleasure," Grandpa said, pulling out a chair between he and Johnny.

"Any word on Jimmy Hackala?" Jenny asked.

"Nothing new," Johnny responded.

"The locals think that R.J., Jimmy's brother, knows where he is, but the cops have him locked up down in Escanaba at a youth detention center." Jenny said.

"Do you know any of them?" Dad asked.

"No," she said, but I talked to some friends from the radio station last night, and they said that R.J. is a local car parts thief who hangs out with some kids from Houghton. They got busted last week stealing a car battery up behind campus. When the boys were arraigned, they found out it was their third or fourth arrest. So, they were automatically sent down to Escanaba Youth Camp for rehab."

"Maybe they'll be able to bring him back to find the brother," Mom offered.

"I don't know, they don't like to make exceptions for habitual offenders," dad said.

"Well, I think this would be a perfect day to take a good look at Hancock and see what kind of town our Johnny has got us involved in," Angie said, pushing herself away from the table.

"If you'd like," Jenny offered, "I can show you the hot spots, and maybe we can catch Helen for lunch."

"That's a wonderful idea Jenny," Angie said.

"Son" dad said, why don't you I and Grandpa, take a look at this old building on Quincy and then see if we can make an appointment to visit Mr. Howard Berg to try and find any common ground to talk about."

"Good idea Dad, I was looking to take a poke at him last night."

"We're not looking to take a poke, Johnny. We're looking to find a Brother in Christ to do some good work in this community," Dad said as they pushed through the door into the parking lot.

"Howard, if you don't get your head out of your armpit, and do something quick, you're going to be the laughing stock of Hancock, Michigan," Maggie whispered into the telephone from Kitty's kitchen. Everybody in town knows that R.J. and Jimmy are your nephews, and with one missing, and one in jail, it makes you look a little foolish. How can you hope to run the city after the next election if you can't even keep track of your own family? Kitty hasn't a clue of what's going on, and if you can't get your cop buddies to bring R.J. back up from Escanaba to help in the search, this is going to drag on and on. I hope he's hiding, and that somebody's helping him, because if he isn't … I've got to go, Kitty's waking up. Do something." (Click)

"I'm cold, Victor," Jimmy said shivering. Lying on the cot in the back room of Victors tool shed reminded him of when he was small, sleeping next to R.J. on those cold nights at the old house in Laurium. Victor's wood stove put out plenty of heat to keep his hands and face warm, but the cold wind blowing between the boards behind him was almost paralyzing his back.

"When do you think I'll be able to go home?" whimpered Jimmy scrunching up in the quilts.

"Oh, don't worry 'bout dat," Victor said. "I got a tarp in da udder shed dat will warm you right up. I'll get it, you go to sleep."

Although Jimmy had been a loner most of his life, this was the first time he could ever remember where life seemed hopeless. He didn't want to spend the rest of his life hiding in this cold filthy old shed, with this weird guy he hardly knew. He wanted to be with R.J. He always took care of him. If R.J. knew how cold he was, he would come and get him and take him away from here right now. Tomorrow he would find his brother. He didn't want to stay with this crazy guy anymore. Victor dragged the big old smelly green tarp in from the other shed and threw it over Jimmy. Jimmy fell asleep wondering if he would ever see his brother again.

CHAPTER 10

"Howard Berg Insurance Agency, Howard speaking."

"Mr. Berg, my name is Reverend John Hendricks, and I am the Senior Pastor of the Central Community church in Grand Rapids. My wife and I drove up yesterday from down state to attend a meeting last night, but instead we were faced with the horrible tragedy of a lost child in your community and this morning I'm being told that this child is your nephew. Is this true?"

"Yes sir, I'm afraid it is," Howard replied, not sure of what was going on.

"Well believe me sir, my family as well as our entire congregation is praying for the safe and speedy return of this young man to your family."

"Thank you, Reverend," Howard said.

"I had originally hoped to discuss a project with you that I thought would benefit you as well as your fine community. I was talking earlier this week with an associate in Lansing about a new program affecting juvenile incarceration camps in your area, but the telephone is no place to discuss such matters. Maybe you would allow me to take you to lunch and discuss some possibilities you might not be aware of," Dad said, nodding at Grandpa.

"I believe I am free for lunch," Howard said hesitantly.

"Name the time and the place, and I'll be there, Howard," John said. "I'm sorry, May I call you Howard?" John pressed.

"Of course, of course John, let's make it the Lakeside Steak House at 1:00"

"See you there, Howard."

John had to adjust his vision as he led his dad and son into the darkened main dining room of the restaurant. The place was decorated with plush carpeting and heavy wooden beams, typical of the steak house genre of the 60's. Howard waved from a corner table, and the Hendricks clan navigated their way towards the back of the dining room.

"You must be John," Howard said rising to shake the outstretched hand.

"And this is my dad, John Senior, and perhaps you may already know my son, Johnny."

Howard smiled weakly at Johnny as they sat next to each other at the table. As the waitress poured waters, and passed out menus, the men discussed the moderating temperatures outside the restaurant. When the drink orders were taken, the waitress left.

"Howard we're really grateful that you consented to see us on such short notice," John said. "I know the stress of having a family member missing, as well as being a business leader and a member of local government must be pressing on your time."

Before Howard could respond the waitress brought the drinks, took the food orders and left. "Howard, the distinguished gentleman sitting across from you is also the Senior Pastor of one of the largest churches in the City of Grand Rapids. He has left his busy schedule to come 600 miles north to join me in a project that is important to both of us. My son Johnny is the reason we are here today."

Howard sat quietly, stirring the ice in his Coke. "Gentlemen, I can appreciate the importance of this project to the three of you, but you have to understand that you can't just fly into a town and expect everybody to change their way of doing things. We've been doing things pretty well for a long time without any outsiders driving 600 miles to try to tell us what we're doing wrong. I don't mean to be rude, but that's the way it looks to us."

The food was served, and the discussion was temporarily suspended while the four men began eating their lunch.

"Howard," John finally said, "I built my first church in the heart of the old town area of Grand Rapids a number of years ago. My wife, Angie, and I were young and enthusiastic, and felt that God had a plan and we were called to do a job. Well, you can imagine we ran up against a stone wall, because no one in the area cared about our vision of our God. They only cared about what they knew, and what they had."

John took a sip of water.

"So, we moved into the neighborhood and opened up a soup kitchen and a babysitting service. Then Angie, being fluent in both English and Spanish, started writing letters for people who couldn't write, and driving mothers to doctors appointments. Next came the storefront church with my guitar for music, and now it is one of the largest churches in Grand Rapids. Howard we are not here to change your community. We are only here to do what Christ asks us to do. We don't want to take over the Aho Building. We want to be on your team. We want to work for you. We just want to help. Does that make any sense?"

"John, you've got to understand," Howard said in frustration, "we just don't do things that way around here. I can't make decisions like that on my own. The council would have my hide. These things take time."

"Mr. Berg" Johnny said, "I know I'm the one that started this negative confrontation by shooting off my big mouth at City Hall, and I apologize for putting you in this difficult position, but you have my word that I will work closely with you to learn how things are done in Hancock, if you will just give me a chance, sir."

John looked at his son with a new respect, and then looked Howard in the eyes.

"This is obviously too big of a decision to make over lunch, but maybe there is room for optimism." John reached his hand across the table, bowed his head and prayed,

"Father, all we have, and all we are, is because of you. Help us to work together for the common good of the young people of Hancock. Help us to nurture our relationship with this fine man Howard Berg, and please Lord, assist the police in finding Jimmy, Amen."

The tension was released and the four men finished their lunch in good fellowship. As they walked back out into the sunshine, John asked Howard if he could call him later.

"Howard, I'll bet your getting tired of talking to me," John said on the phone, "but I've spent all afternoon with an associate of mine at the Department of Human Services in Lansing concerning your nephew at Bay Pines Camp in Escanaba. Can you meet me at Kaleva's for a cup of coffee? I think I can fill you in on some information that might come in handy."

Howard had already had his supper and said, "I'll see you there in twenty minutes,"

The temperature had dropped thirty degrees since they had left the steak house earlier in the day, and both men bundled up to go to the Coffee Shop. John was sitting in one of the red plastic booths by the front window as

Howard strode through the front door. Catching the waitress's eye, he walked over and shook John's hand.

"I'm all ears," he said, as the waitress approached with two cups and a fresh pot of coffee.

"Howard, I apologize for taking up so much of your time when you obviously have more important family matters that need your attention, but the fact of the matter is, the importance of your position in the community makes you the right person to deal with on this subject, and here's why."

Howard leaned forward and took a sip of coffee.

"Once again, the great State of Michigan, finds itself with all the powers that be stuck down in Lansing, while the necessary resolutions to make this state run smoothly are in the hands of the local communities. Your nephew is a classic example. A small teen problem and a prominent family's name is dragged through the mud by a lack of inter-agency communication. Howard, if it can happen to your family it can happen to anyone. Do you agree?"

Howard wasn't sure what John was talking about, but so far it hadn't cost him anything to listen.

CHAPTER 11

The sky through the window was the color of slate as Jimmy slowly lifted the heavy tarp up over his head. The nauseating smell as well as the coarse texture of the canvas on his skin, had kept him awake in kind of a semi-consciousness. Victor was snoring peacefully in his bunk across the shed, and Burt, his huge German shepherd, lay close to the stove with his paws covering his black snout. Jimmy and Burt had formed a mutual dislike for each other ever since R.J. had dropped him off at Victors, and that was fine by him. But, time was running out, and if Jimmy was ever going to get away and find his brother, this might be his only chance. Quietly he pulled back the covers and slid to the floor. Reaching under the bunk he found his boots and slowly crawled into the next room. Burt lazily opened his eyes and watched him go, but soon returned to his dream. Tying the laces of his old work boots, and pulling an old work jacket off the hook by the side door, he quietly opened it enough to squeeze through and crept out into a fog so thick that he couldn't see two feet in front of him. He had no idea which direction to go or what to do if he ran into anything. He crept outside into a copse of damp hemlock trees. Water dripped on his head. Jimmy just knew he had to run. Everything was wet. He could see his breath blowing from his mouth as he made his way through the rusted junk cars like giant land tortoises in the heavy morning mist. Reaching out in front of him, he felt a fence. With one foot in the snowy muck and his fingers enmeshed in the wire, he lifted his other foot and with all of his strength pulled his body over the top falling to the sloppy ground. "R.J., where are you?" he whimpered. Cold and wet Jimmy dragged himself through the fog until he reached a dirt road. Climbing the small bank on his hands and knees, he finally stood up. Jimmy turned left and came to a railroad track with rusty rails. He could feel the metal rails under his feet and knew which way the road went, but which way should he go? He stopped and listened. Water was dripping from nearby branches and a song bird was singing not ten feet away in the dense fog. As he turned toward the comforting sound, the snap of a three inch dead branch echoed from across the road followed by the sound of a bear rutting in the brush. Jimmy froze. Everything he had heard or learned about Michigan black bears flashed through his mind. If only he had a weapon, he thought. Maybe he could find a stick, or a big rock. Maybe he could hide. Tears started running down his cheeks. He was hiding. He couldn't even see his feet.

"AAAARGH," the bear roared, seeming closer, splashing water and throwing great chunks of something.

Run, Jimmy thought, but which way? Left, Right, down the tracks? *Where was R.J.? This was all his fault.* The bear roared again, and Jimmy took off down the road like a shot.

Running with his hands out in front of him to protect his face, crying like a baby. He ran right by Victor's front gate, hopefully heading towards Baraga. With the fog beginning to dissipate, Jimmy dropped his arms, stopped his crying and ran faster.

Jerry Godwin, school bus driver for Baraga Elementary School District, was just pulling away from one of his stops when a loud thump on the side of the bus caused him to hit the brakes. The fog had blown back in and was so thick he thought a deer might have run into the side of the bus. He engaged the red blinkers, exited the bus and found the young boy the whole county was looking for lying on the side of the road covered in mud, unconscious.

CHAPTER 12

"Yes sir I know who you are, but doctor's orders are that only immediate family are allowed in the room, and that does not include uncles." The nurse dressed in a multicolored smock using her clipboard and her cold smile as a shield prevented Uncle Howard from entering Jimmy's room.

The Mining Gazette, as well as Channel 6 News out of Marquette, had been covering the story of Jimmy Hackala's miraculous reappearance. All attempts by news agencies to gain more information about Jimmy's whereabouts had been thwarted by the attending doctors and legal representatives protecting the minor. His condition was being monitored on an hourly basis, and so far he was still unconscious. Rumors of collusion between his older brother R.J. and other unsavory characters in the auto theft business were bandied about around the area, but until Jimmy's condition improved the police and the news media could only sit and wait.

"The Hendricks clan was forced to return to Grand Rapids to fulfill their responsibilities, but assured Johnny that they were confident that his work would unfold in God's time and that they were pleased with his efforts and progress. John continued to monitor the situation with R.J. in Escanaba, and to confer with his contacts in Lansing working towards a way to put the older Hackala boy back in Hancock closer to his brother and mother. It seemed to John that if Howard would agree to help promote Johnny's Aho Building Youth Mission, perhaps he could create a council made up of representatives of the Hancock City Council, the Bay Pines Youth Camp, the Michigan State Police, and the Houghton-Hancock Clergy Association. Then maybe, just maybe, they could get R.J. placed on a restricted parole or tether program in Hancock.

As John sat in his office staring out the window at a cold November day, he wasn't even sure that some five hundred miles away to the north, R.J. even cared.

Johnny side-kicked the fresh snow with the edge of his new boots as he climbed the rickety steps, cleaning off the railing as he went. Six inches of new white powder had covered Hancock while everyone slept and with the exception of the snow plows, very few had made the effort to clear off their sidewalks and porches. Johnny peered through the small door window panes for any sign of life. Seeing none, he took off his glove and gave the cold glass a rap. Stomping his feet to gain a little warmth, and hopefully rouse somebody inside, he again banged on the door.

"Hold your horses," shouted a desperate voice from inside, as a bleary eyed Kitty angrily yanked open the door.

"Do you know what time it is?" she gasped sucking in a mouth full of cold air.

"I'm sorry. Please forgive me for waking you up. I know this is a terrible time for you. Maybe we could talk later."

"What do you want? You're the new kid I read about in the paper. What's going on?" She asked confused.

"I saw you on the local news last night, and the terrible way everyone was badgering you. I went up to the hospital chapel and spent the night praying for Jimmy, and this morning I'm here to help you."

Kitty's eyes softened, "How is he?"

"They wouldn't let me see him, but the nurse at the station said he looked very peaceful, even though he's in a coma."

"Yeah, that's the way he was when I left him yesterday. They don't know what's going on with his head, but his body's okay. Say, its cold out here, why don't you come in for a second," she said, holding the door open.

Johnny entered the living room and was embarrassed by the state of disarray, but Kitty didn't even notice.

"If you'd like," Johnny offered, "I could come back in an hour, pick you up and take you up to see Jimmy."

"Would you do that?"

"I'll be here in exactly one hour and we'll go together."

"It's a deal," she said, and Johnny made his way to the door.

Miia Virtenen

Miia Virtenen was a shadow. For eighteen years she was the door mat for everyone who needed one. Her verbally abusive father, Matia, who stumbled through life an unfulfilled wood pulper in the timber industry, went from the chain saw to the beer bottle. Her mother, Vilma, kept Miia from finding any peace at home by blaming her for all of life's shortcomings. Miia was small and all of the Nordic attributes so often attributed to her heritage were lost in her genetics. Her hair was thin and mousey. Her complexion was bad from childhood, and consequently blotchy and unpleasant. Her posture from constant physical and mental abuse made her seem like she was always cowering, or backing up. She only had two defenders in her whole life. One was her brother Norman who quit school and joined the Army to get away from the family. The other was R.J. Hackala, who beat up on people who disrespected her. All through the years they were in school together, for reasons unknown to her, he protected her. She never understood the relationship, but he always made her feel very special. He was never her friend, just her protector. Being a loner she was very secretive in her own space and her possessions, and protective of everything she personally deemed important. She had a full time housekeeping job at Portage Health Hospital on the afternoon shift, and cleaned up and stocked Rudy's bar four days a week during the day time. In exchange Rudy let her stay for free in the little two room apartment up above the bar. The arrangement was a good deal for both her and Rudy, and also kept her busy. More importantly it allowed her to keep tabs on her one alleged responsibility, the Hackalas.

"Good morning, Mrs. Hackala," said the nurse looking up from her desk.

"Good morning, Bella," replied Kitty breezily, how's Jimmy.

"About the same I'd say," responded the nurse looking at the chart.

"This is my Pastor, Reverend Hendricks; He'll be going in with me this morning."

"I think that will be fine," said the nurse.

Little Jimmy lay curled in the fetal position peacefully sleeping as they entered the darkened room. "The little bugger looks like such an angel all curled up like a baby. I could ring his neck for all the trouble he's put us all through," she smiled running her hand through his hair, "What do you think he's thinking about, Pastor? I hope you don't mind me calling you my Pastor. I really don't have one, and it's kind of nice to think that maybe there is some one who really cares about us, at least a little."

"Kitty, think about this. God and Jesus, and all of the angels in the universe, are praying for you, Jimmy and R.J. right now. Here, take my hands, and let's join them.

> *"Precious Father we bid you good morning and thank you for this wonderful day. Kitty and I are so very grateful that you have chosen us to stand watch over this precious child and breathe love and hope into his wounded body. Give him the miracle he needs, Father and restore him in full measure to the person we know he can be. We ask a blessing for brother R.J. stuck in youth camp in Escanaba. Change his heart, Father. He has such a long life to live. Help him to see your light. And finally, wrap your arms around Kitty, Lord. You have given her a full load and she needs your help to see her way through. All these things we ask in your Son Jesus' name Amen."*

Kitty opened her eyes with tears streaming down her face. "Do you think any of that stuff's gonna happen?" she asked, blowing her nose.

"Do I think that God creates miracles, and makes thing better, and heals the sick, and releases the prisoners? Kitty, of course he does. He brought us together in prayer, didn't he? He's taken your young son from the unknown to a safe hospital bed, didn't He? Let me ask you something,

Kitty? For taking your two sons out of harms way, what has He asked for in return? What's the price tag? What do you owe Him right now?" Johnny sat across from her in one of those big yellow overstuffed chairs.

"I give up," she smiled, what?"

"Nothing."

"Why's that?"

"Because He loves you."

"I wouldn't bet on that," she smiled uncomfortably wondering what in the world he was talking about.

They relaxed and chatted for a while and Johnny told her about this great little bakery down the hill on Quincy that had Thimbleberry tarts, and she said she would rather have sausage and eggs, so they prayed again for Jimmy, she kissed him on the forehead and they left the hospital. After breakfast Johnny dropped off Kitty and went back to Helen's place.

"Hi, how are you?" Johnny asked a teenager sitting on the front steps.

"Fine."

"Are you looking for Mrs. Aho?"

"No."

"Can I help you?" Johnny continued the interrogation.

"I know R.J."

"My name's Johnny, what's yours?"

"Miia."

"'Miia, that's a pretty name,' Johnny said as he sat down on the step next to her.

"Are you a friend of R.J.'s" Johnny asked.

"R.J. don't have no friends. Never did; never will."

"Why do you say that?"

"Cause he don't trust nobody."

"How about Jimmy?"

"That's different."

"Why."

"Cause Jimmy's his brother, and Jimmy depends on him."

"Who does R.J. depend on?"

"R.J."

There was a long pause while the two stared across the street toward the ravine and the lake. Miia looked at Johnny. "R.J. steals stuff."

"'What kind of stuff."

"They break into cars."

"Where do you live Miia?

"Over Rudy's bar."

"I think we need to talk to a friend of mine," Johnny said, pulling out his telephone.

"Hello, this is Johnny Hendricks, I'd like to speak to Tom Martin, please."

"Speaking. How are you doing, Johnny?"

"Fine, Tom. I just met a young lady who is very interested helping the Hackala family. She has known R.J. most of her life and may have some back ground information that might help us. We are presently at Helen Aho's place down on Navy, west of Dakota. Are you tied up?"

"I'm on my way, Johnny" Tom said.

Miia explained her unique school relationship with R.J. and also how she had occasionally met Jimmy wandering around Hancock, but he had no idea who she was. She on the other hand knew Jimmy was R.J.'s kid brother and was aware that Kitty was tending bar at Rudy's.

Tom Martin's unmarked police car pulled to the curb, and the officer got out. Johnny introduced Tom to Miia and the three walked to an old picnic table by the galvanized railing across the street.

"Miia, I don't want you to betray any confidences, but there may be some very bad people around who might want to hurt little Jimmy, and we can use all the help we can get. What can you tell us?"

"Well, I was just telling Johnny that I've known R.J. most of my life and I see Jimmy every day." She volunteered.

"How do you see Jimmy every day?" Tom asked.

"I work in housekeeping at the Portage Health Hospital so I'm able to pretty much keep an eye on him on a daily basis, but what I wanted to tell you was that Jimmy's been running loose for quite a while. I don't think R.J. or Kitty have any idea what he's been up to. He stops and talks to me when I'm cleaning the bar during the day. You know, Kitty tends bar at night, and I think Jimmy feels like this is part of his life here because she doesn't have time for him in hers. It's kind of crazy, you know," Miia said looking across the street towards the lake. "It's really kind of sad."

"Well, what did he talk about when he visited the bar?" Johnny asked.

"He said some day when he got older he and R.J. were going to get a place for their folks where it was warm all the time and live all together," she answered.

Johnny and Tom looked at each other without reacting to the thought.

"Did he say what R.J. did with his time?" Tom asked.

"R.J. and some friends dealt in auto parts, and they made good money." She said.

"Did Jimmy ever say where they did this business?" Johnny asked.

"All around the area I guess. Some guy helped them sell the parts that they got, but I don't know who. I think he's older," Miia suggested.

"What makes you think that?" Tom asked.

"Oh, just the way R.J. talked like he was in a bigger business." Jimmy had told her.

"But he never mentioned a name," Tom said.

"No, never." She said curtly.

"Where did Jimmy go after he left the bar?" Johnny asked.

"Sometimes I would make him a sandwich from the cooler, and we would sit outside in the sunshine. Other times he would wander around town, and once he told me he would sneak back into the house and hide in the basement until his mother went to work. He just had no place to go or no one to go to. Sometimes at night when I go into his room in the hospital, I watch him, and I think the reason he doesn't wake up is that he has no place to go to. It's really kind of sad," she said lifting one of her bangs behind her ear.

Johnny thanked her and Tom offered her a ride up to Rudy's, but Miia said the walk would be good exercise.

As Johnny and Tom stared at Portage Lake, they thought about stolen auto parts, lost boys of all ages and the futility of too little too late in the lives of so many people.

Victor and his dog, Burt, sat in the parking lot of the Hill Top Restaurant in L'ance, looking down the hill at where it had all started. He was an old man now and his life was behind him. If he had made mistakes, they were mistakes taught to him by people who had done the best they could in the times they lived in. He could vividly remember the fire and the fear he had felt running away from the Nazi haters, but the decisions that were made by others who knew more were decisions he was forced to abide by. He loved Ralph and Eileen like they were his own parents, and was grateful for all they had taught him and the inheritance they had given him. His only regrets were in leaving his junk yard, the only home he had ever had, and knowing that young Jimmy was seriously hurt, and that he was partly to blame. Victor learned long ago that life was full of trials and misfortunes.

Yesterday he had gone to Marquette. He sold his car crusher and parts business for cash to his silent partner and returned last night. He burned any incriminating evidence, and went to the big rock, dug up his inheritance and locked the front gate to VICTOR WURTZS' JUNKYARD AND AUTO PARTS for the last time. Burt climbed into the camper, and Victor drove up the hill and slept out behind the Hill Top Motel to wait for morning. He had never been anywhere but the Copper country, but thought now might be a good time to do a little traveling, especially where it was warmer.

CHAPTER 13

R.J. stretched out on his bed in his one man room. All things considered, it was probably the best accommodations he had ever had, except for the fact that his world had been turned upside down. He had been told that his brother was missing, and it was all he could do to keep from laughing in the faces of the State Police who had come to question him about Jimmy's possible whereabouts. *So, suddenly everybody's concerned; everybody wants to help the poor Hackala family. Well, it seems like they're a little too late*, he thought.

"Still no change," Officer Miles said, sticking his head into R.J.'s room. Jimmy had rolled over yesterday, and the doctor's thought that was an encouraging sign, but nothing since.

"Are you sure you don't want to call your mother, or any other family members?" asked the detention camp guard.

R.J. just smiled at Officer Miles. Actually, for the first time in his life, he was scared to death. He had lost control. He wasn't the boss. Jimmy might die, or never wake up. There wasn't anything he could do about it. It wasn't Victor's fault, either, and yet if Jimmy woke up and spoke Victor's name, Victor might go to prison for a long time. *Some how I've got to get out of here,* he thought.

Although Bay Pines Youth Detention Camp was a forty bed center for restricted non felons awaiting court decisions, it was based inside of a State Penitentiary with full security with barbed wire fences. This was information that R.J. was unaware of when he decided to try and escape that evening to fix the situation up in Hancock. Escaping the billets wasn't a problem, but when he got to the fence with the razor wire on top, he suddenly realized he was in over his head. When the police from Hancock had driven him through the front gate to admit him, he hadn't paid any attention to the security surrounding the facility. All he had on was his orange prison jump suit and a pair of slip on canvas loafers when he left his room, and now he was outside in sub freezing temperatures and facing a twelve foot fence with razored concertina wire on top. He looked around and saw nobody, and ran back to his room for a blanket. Crouching down and looking in both directions, he began scaling the fence with the blanket wrapped around his shoulders to prevent him from being seen, and to throw over the razor sharp wire when he got to the top. While trying to lay the blanket on the sharp wires he slipped setting off the alarms. In flailing trying to escape he cut his wrist so badly on the wire he nearly bled to death before the guards could cut him down.

As the EMS rushed him to the infirmary he broke down in tears crying Jimmy's name. There was no doubt that R.J. wanted to die right there. He couldn't take it anymore. He was tired of always being responsible for everybody and he just wanted out. He just wanted to be free.

At 6:00 am Kitty called Johnny instead of Howard and by 7:30 they were on the road to Escanaba. The sun and the mist were rising off of Pike Bay as they drove through Chassell, and Kitty was numb as she laid with her head on the cold passenger window glass trying to get some relief from her inner pain.

"Johnny, I don't know what to say," Kitty whispered, all cried out. "I don't know who he is. He's my own son. I've never really known him. He's so much like Robert he scares me, and now this. What am I supposed to do?"

"Kitty, you're not supposed to do anything. You're just supposed to be there. Let God do the healing. Let God open up two hearts that are hurting and confused and try and find a little peace." Three hours later they were pulling through security at the Prison.

The nurse led Kitty and Johnny into the ward where R.J. lay cuffed to a bed with his right arm stitched and bandaged. R.J.'s eyes were closed and he was motionless.

"Honey, it's your mother. Are you okay?" Kitty asked with little feeling.

"Go away," R.J. said without moving or opening his eyes.

"R.J. don't be that way. We drove all the way down here just to help you." Kitty said, beginning to feel a little anger that R.J. didn't appreciate what she had done.

"You've never done anything that wasn't for Kitty, now go." R.J. started to rise up and tears started to run down his face from the pain in his heart and in his arm. He fell back down on the bed and began sobbing and Kitty stood there powerless to help a son who had never asked for anything from her.

Kitty leaned on the railing and began wailing with an empty heart next to R.J. The nurse rushed over from tending another patient. Johnny stopped her and explained that this reunion was long overdue, and to let them go, and she did.

"Kitty continued weeping, saying, "I'm so sorry, please forgive me. R.J. please forgive me. I've been such a terrible mother. Can you and Jimmy ever forgive me?"

The two sobbed themselves into exhaustion until they both squeezed each others hands. Words weren't possible, but Kitty ran her fingers through R.J.'s hair as she must have when he was a child, and slowly old memories and feelings entered two last souls.

Johnny came around the bed and put his hands around theirs and bowed his head:

*"Most gracious God, You have taken two lonely
hearts, and raised them up to your glory, and for*

that we are very grateful. We ask nothing more than to allow this mother and son to learn to love each other and help to heal brother Jimmy and create a loving family. Amen."

"R.J., this is Johnny. He's my new pastor." Kitty said through bleary eyes.

R.J. just laid there in complete exhaustion while Kitty straightened his sheets. She felt a new purpose in life as Johnny scooted her out the door so the nurse could calm R.J. and redress his wound.

"It's a miracle," Kitty said as they sat in the waiting room, "just like you said."

"I didn't say it would be a miracle, I said let God do his will, and now let's get some lunch and let R.J. rest up and we'll visit him this afternoon. Kitty was all smiles as they drove out the gate towards downtown Escanaba.

"Hi mom, how's life in G.R.?" Johnny asked Angie while seated in a booth at Rosey's Diner.

"Fine son. Where are you calling from?" "Kitty and I are down in Escanaba visiting R.J., and there have been some new developments. Is Dad around?"

"Yes, I'll get him."

Johnny took a mouthful of Rosey's Corned Beef Hash Special just as Dad came on the line.

"Hi Johnny. What's going on?"

"Well, I'm giving you a heads up on the latest episode of our soap opera."

Dad took notes on all that had happened concerning the Hackala family, and repeated it to Johnny. "Does that sound about right, son?"

"Yes sir, I think that's exactly where we stand." Johnny said.

"If you have any suggestions, I'm all ears," Dad said.

"I think it all depends on what R.J. has to say. I think he knows more about Jimmy's disappearance than he's telling us. So, until he comes clean there's nothing we can present to the police. I'm going to talk with him after lunch and see if I can convince him that it will benefit his whole family to tell what he knows."

"Let's hope so, son. Keep in touch. Bye for now."

Johnny and Kitty finished their lunch and drove back to Bay Pines.

When Johnny and Kitty returned to the Infirmary ward, R.J.'s bed was empty. The nurse said that R.J. had requested a telephone call and had been escorted by an officer to the phone bank. Kitty and Johnny sat by the bed and waited. Ten minutes later R.J. returned with his arm in a sling followed by a female officer who chained him to the bed. R.J. still wasn't ready to look Kitty or Johnny in the face.

"Honey, we brought you a piece of pecan pie. I know that used to be your favorite," Kitty said as she handed him the Styrofoam box and plastic spoon.

R.J. took the pie with his wrapped hand and unlocked the top with the fork.

"I guess you heard Jimmy's doing a little better. Pastor Johnny and I stopped and saw him yesterday and he looks like a little angel, doesn't he?" she said nodding towards Johnny.

"Where'd you come from anyway?' R.J. asked Johnny tersely, lowering his spoon.

"I'm brand new in town, R.J. With all the excitement we haven't had a chance to properly meet."

"What are you doing with my mother?" R.J. said without emotion.

"R.J., I'm doing everything I possibly can to get you transferred out of Bay Pines and back up to Hancock and into some sort of parole situation to help your mom and your kid brother."

"Why?" There was an angry silence between the two men.

"Because you won't," Johnny said looking R.J. straight in the eyes.

"How do you expect me to do anything chained to a bed," R.J. stuck out his chin with that half grin that always got him in trouble.

"The first thing you can do is to tell your mother whether you were running away when you were hanging on that fence last night, or whether you were running towards your brother Jimmy to try and help him." The cocky smile was gone. "And secondly, you can tell us who you made the phone call to just now, and start helping us to understand what's been happening to that little boy lying in a coma worrying about his big brother."

R.J. put the half eaten pie down on the night stand and looked away. "You wouldn't understand. Neither one of you."

"Is this the part where you tell us you had it so bad that the only thing you could do was steal car parts from some hard working people and sell them to some other loser, who probably sells them for pennies on the dollar to support a drug habit. Is that his story too? And when they send both of you down to Marquette Prison for the rest of your lives you can look at each other and say, aw, you wouldn't understand. R.J. are you really that stupid? Can you really believe that if your kid brother ever gains consciousness again, he won't be right behind you? And your mother will tend bar for the rest of her life and her ex husband, a drunk, and her two sons in prison for life. Is that the best you can do? Can you look your mother in the eye and tell her that's the best she can expect out of her oldest son? Come on give me his name!"

"Victor," R.J. said, tears running down his face. Everyone in the ward stood motionless except for the police officer who picked up her phone.

Once R.J. started talking the story flowed like a river. It had started two years ago when one of the older kids he hung out with showed him how to steal boat batteries from fishing boats tied to the docks in the surrounding lakes. R.J. made five dollars a piece, and for a sixteen- year-old that added up. Then, one day he got to ride along down to Baraga and he met Victor.

Victor told him he was a smart kid and there was big money to be made in the parts business.

So, next he learned cars and trucks, catalytic converters and radios. He even stole a small boat on a trailer. The longer he talked, the deeper the hole he dug for himself.

The State Police had both ends of the Baraga Plains Road blocked off with no sirens or blinkers flashing. It was a cold windy afternoon, as they proceeded on foot. As they neared the fenced corners on each end of the road, armed troops were dispersed around the perimeter. A state helicopter was armed and ready in the Baraga Ojibwa Casino parking lot if needed. At exactly 2:00 p.m. an armored vehicle proceeded south on the Plains Road toward the VICTOR WURTZ AUTO PARTS AND JUNK YARK sign and made a left hand turn down into a sandy drive and a padlocked front gate. The command was given at the road block, and the armored vehicle smashed through the gate followed by state, county and township vehicles which drove all around the property ending at the big shed in the middle. Tom Martin with a bull horn ordered Victor Wurtz to come out with his hands in the air, but all that could be heard was a song bird singing from the limb of a white birch tree above the shed. Maybe the same bird Jimmy heard a couple of weeks before.

After it was established that there was no kidnapping involved, and in fact R.J. was simply trying to protect his brother, the F.B.I. bowed out of the case. The crime scene investigators went over the junk yard with backhoes and sniffing dogs, but found that Victor was at least two steps ahead of them. When they discovered that the deed to the property had just changed hands from Mr. Wurtz to some shady organization with high profile lawyers and connections all over the country, it was obvious that the best Houghton County could do was go after young R.J. Hackala. The next day the Michigan State Attorney General found himself on the 6:00 p.m. news in Lansing being questioned about a case in the U.P. After a phone call was made, the next day R.J. Hackala, criminal extraordinaire, was once again back in a holding cell in downtown Houghton talking to Officer Danny Johnson.

"Good morning, R.J.," said Danny rocking on his heels. "I hope the accommodations are acceptable."

"They're fine," R.J. responded quietly.

"Excuse me," said Danny leaning in as if he hadn't heard correctly.

"I said they're fine," said R.J. said looking straight at Danny.

"What happened?" Danny asked confused.

"To what,"

"To you, that cocky kid we sent down to Escanaba. When you fell off the fence did you bump your head, like your kid brother," Danny laughed. "I mean, you're not the same. Where's that cocky, spit in your eye R.J. Hackala that's been driving us crazy for the last couple of years. You've lost your fire, boy. You look like they beat you down. I don't believe it." Danny walked back into the squad room to chat with the other officers.

R.J. spent the whole trip back from Escanaba trying to figure out his next move. He knew his future was out of his hands. His two partners in crime had gotten together with their lawyers and blamed him for everything and pled to a reduced sentence, so he had the target directly on his back. The only thing that might save him was the fact that he was still a juvenile, but the fact that he was a habitual offender left his future up in the air. He hoped that Jimmy was okay and that Victor had gotten away, but other than that life was on hold. He wasn't sure who that praying dude was with his mother, but he probably could use a few of those too.

CHAPTER 14

"Howard Berg Insurance Agency, Howard speaking."

"John Hendricks down in Grand Rapids, Howard, how are things up in "Copper Country?""

"Quite frankly John, I don't know. If you're talking about the weather, I'd say it's been better. If you're talking about the Hackala family, I'd say it's the same as the weather. Jimmy's still resting peacefully, R.J. is still rotting in his cell, and Kitty and Maggie have taken a shine to that son of yours, and are planning all sorts of "do gooder" projects with a bunch of preachers. Now, if you're asking about me, I'm just sitting here twiddling my thumbs waiting for Christmas."

"Well, Howard, maybe I've got something that will cheer you up a little.

My contact in Lansing says that the Attorney General is getting unfavorable mail from down state about not enough money and police presence being used in high crime areas in lower Michigan and all the news media wants to talk about is a petty thief in Hancock with a sick brother. My friend asked how we can make it go away and here's what I proposed." John ran over the details of is plan with Howard and said goodbye.

"Hancock City Hall, how may I help you?" asked Penny.

"This is John Hendricks calling from Grand Rapids. I wonder if I might speak to Bob Heikinen, please."

"Of course you can, Mr. Hendricks," Penny said pleasantly, "Hold please."

"Is this my friend from the land of the wooden shoe," asked Bob, noting John's Dutch heritage.

"If this is my friend from the land of the pastie," John replied, and both men had a chuckle. "Bob I think I have some good news."

The next call was to Johnny who in turn called Father Walt, and a preliminary meeting was set for two nights later in the Hancock council room. In attendance were Bob Heikinen, Howard Berg, Bertha Mittila, Father Walter, Chief of Police Tom Burley, Detective Tom Martin, Captain Jenifer Townley from Bay Pines, and Johnny.

"I'd like to thank you all for coming out on such a lousy evening. What we're attempting to do might have far reaching effects on the future of troubled youths in our state," Bob Heikinen said as he went around the table and greeted each attendee. When he got to Johnny he said, "If you don't already know this young man, he is the 'Joker' in the deck, Johnny Hendricks," and everybody smiled. "The reason I say he is the 'Joker', is that if it weren't for him, we wouldn't be here. I think we need to hear his story to fully understand how we got to where we are tonight so that we can collectively formulate a plan to present to the state representative next Tuesday afternoon."

Bob took his seat and everyone focused on what Johnny had to say. When he finished, Bob took over again.

"I've taken the liberty to ask Bertha to take minutes and run the chalk board for us this evening. I think if we can collect our ideas and thoughts, and present them in a uniform fashion it may help us to formulate a plan to show the folks down state that we are serious and of one mind in our dealing with this situation. If you look around the table, I think you'll agree that we represent a pretty broad cross section of the leadership in Hancock. Now, it's important to remember that Johnny's proposal is completely civil in purpose, and by that I mean that although it is supported by church organizations and partially funded by churches, it is totally separated from any particular church doctrine. So, for those of you who represent police organizations, you will not be tangling with church and state issues. Are we clear?"

"Not to interrupt," said Jennifer from Bay Pines, "but why are we hugging this particular perp? I mean, we in the law enforcement business have put away a lot nicer kids than this, for a lot less." The cops all suppressed a smile, as if it were an inside joke.

"Let me try and tackle that one," said Johnny. "If I gave all three of you law enforcers ten 'get out of jail free cards', for ten youths in your past that you thought might have been better served by a program like this as opposed to incarceration, would you, if the opportunity existed have opted for another alternative."

Father Walter winked at Johnny, and Jennifer said, "This kid should have been a lawyer," and everybody burst out laughing.

"In the short time I have lived in Hancock, I have learned what the residents have known their whole lives. No one below the bridge gives a hoot about what goes on up here and unless we find a way to help ourselves, we can expect no help from the trolls," Johnny said in all seriousness. "I am not ashamed to admit that my coming to Hancock was a personal calling from God. I have a feeling that everyone in this room has had a similar calling to try and make something, or some place better when you took up your current positions in the community, so our motives are not so different. So to me, the plus side of this situation is that together, maybe we can collectively help out one messed-up family. And, hopefully straighten out one perp and his kid brother. If together we can create a community youth council to meet periodically and work together to stop the wayward kids before they get in too deep, maybe all of our lives will benefit. A representative from the state government has agreed to meet with us on Tuesday in the Council Hall in Gaylord. If we have a solid proposal to deal with youth offenders they may give us the green light to go ahead as a trial program, with R.J. as a test case. They want him off the front page of the newspapers down-state, and they want us to punish him nicely and quietly. They would be even happier if in the future we could come up with something pre-emptive, sanctioned by local law enforcement and community government to act as a safety net to keep these things from getting out of hand."

"Wow," said Tom Martin, "that's a pretty tall order. If this is so easy why isn't everybody around the country doing it?"

"I'm sure they are Tom," said Father Walter, "maybe not on a national level, or city-wide in larger metropolitan areas, but YMCAs, church youth clubs, 4H Clubs in rural areas, even Boy Scouts, and Girl Scouts, all share in helping to get children to socially adjust. It's the ones that fall through the cracks that get lost and need the most help, and that's the safety net we're talking about."

"And who's going to start something like that?" asked Tom Martin.

"Johnny," said Howard, and everyone looked at the boy from Grand Rapids.

Johnny looked at Howard. "Are you saying that you would support a youth mission in Hancock?"

"If you would lead it," Howard said.

"Would the Aho Building be available if it passes inspection?" Johnny asked Bob.

"As soon as we can get it ready," Bob Heikinen said smiling.

"If we all agree that this is the right course of action to deal with the state reps on Tuesday afternoon," Johnny asked looking around the table, "I have one more request."

"And that is?" asked Bob.

"I would like to nominate Howard Berg to be the President and lead representative of the Hancock Youth Council and Mission Project, and to represent us in Gaylord. Would you lead us Howard?" asked Johnny.

"It would be a privilege," said Howard smugly.

More suggestions and proposals were made, and Bertha competently registered them in their proper places on the chalk board until there was some semblance of order. Howard asked Johnny if he would go with him on Tuesday and all agreed that would be a great idea. Before Howard brought the meeting to a close, Johnny asked if it would be out of order if he offered up a prayer for Jimmy and the success of their program.

"Dear Lord, we are all amazed how easy life becomes when You are in our presence. We ask for a healing for young Jimmy, Father, It is time he came back to us to retake his place in our world. Be with his brother R.J. and open his heart and help him to understand that his whole life is ahead of him, and thank you for a

wonderful evening with good people doing good
work. Amen."

The eight friends left City Hall as Bertha turned out the lights and locked the door.

"Johnny, have you got a minute," Howard said, as they walked towards their cars.

"Sure Howard, is everything all right?" Johnny asked.

"Well, things have been better. Maggie's not herself lately."

"I'm sorry to hear that, is she ill?" Johnny asked. "Hey it's kind of cold, why don't you jump in my van and we'll get a coffee."

"Thanks I'd like that. Nah, she's not sick, at least she's not physically sick, I think she's just sick of me. She moved in with her sister. Would you believe it, after all the problems that family has caused me, she has the audacity to move in with that drunk."

"Howard, I'm sorry. When did this happen?"

"When you and Kitty came back from Escanaba and they brought back R.J."

"What was her reason for moving out?"

"She said she thought Kitty might try and kill herself. You don't think she will do you?"

"Boy I hope not, but she doesn't have it easy. How about you, Howard, don't you feel a lot of stress? I mean your life has been turned upside down with no relief in sight, at least until tonight. It must make you angry that you had nothing to do with any of this, and now you're wife has moved out. How do you cope?"

"You want to know the truth? Can I trust you not to tell anyone?"

"Of course Howard."

"I think I'm dying."

"Why do you think that?"

"My stomach's all cramped up. Sometimes I pass blood. I can't keep any food down. I take all kinds of medicine, but it doesn't do any good. I think I'm a goner."

"Howard, can I pray for you?" Johnny asked.

"I'm not going to die tonight. I'm just dying that's all."

"Do you believe in prayer?"

'Believe me, I didn't get this far in life by praying for what ever I wanted, I got up every morning and went out and worked for it. Nothing ever came easy for old Howard Berg. I can tell you that. You know, Maggie had it way too easy growing up, and I gave her everything she wanted and now look what she's done to me. She thinks she can embarrass me in front of the whole community. Well, she's got another thing coming if she thinks old Howard's going to lay down and let that drunk and those two brats walk all over my reputation." Howard pounded the dash, threw open the door, and strutted towards his car. Johnny could see that Howard was too wound up to reason with so he let him drive off. It was still early in the evening, and the weather was moderating so he thought he would drive over to Houghton and see if maybe R.J. might consent to a little visit. He hadn't seen him since Escanaba and thought that maybe it was time to break the ice on a personal level and see if he could eliminate a little anger. Johnny drove down South Avenue past the Court House to the Sheriff's Office and the lock-up.

"Good evening Officer," said Johnny stomping the slush off his boots.

"Good evening to you, Mr. Hendricks," responded Ron Burch, on desk duty.

"Do I know you?" Johnny asked with a smile.

"No sir you don't, but everybody knows you," said Ron returning the smile.

'Well, I don't know if that's good or bad." said Johnny.

"In your case it's good. My wife says you've come to save the Keweenaw. My name's Ron Burch."

"I'm Johnny Hendricks, Ron, and you tell your wife that we can use all the help we can get from everybody. Ron, I don't know if you can help me, but I've come to try and see R.J. I don't know if he'll even talk to me, but there are a lot of things at stake involving his future. I was hoping I might talk to him to get some idea what he's thinking. Now if it's against the rules, I'll understand, but if there's a chance it might help a lot of people."

"I'm not sure he'll talk to anyone, Johnny, he's really been belligerent, but I think he's just scared. He's in there by himself tonight, right through that door to the left." Johnny walked down the short hallway to the holding cell where the prisoner sat on the end of his bunk staring at the wall.

"R.J., I was up to see Jimmy this afternoon, and I got a feeling he needs to see you," Johnny said to the shadow beyond the bars. There was silence coming from the corner where R.J. was sitting. "I'm sorry I bothered you R.J., I'll tell him I saw you." Johnny began walking towards the door.

"Why do you keep bothering us?" said a voice from the shadows.

"That's a pretty good question. It's certainly not for my health. You know there's a Red Wings hockey game on T.V. tonight, and I'm out here in the cold trying to talk to a guy who hates his mother and his brother."

"You know that's not true."

"Tell me what you've done for either one of them lately, my friend. Oh I know, you were stealing car parts for Jimmy's college education, right."

"And I suppose that drunk tending bar all night was doing any better?" R.J. lashed out.

"You know, I don't think she's any happier with the way things have worked out than you are. Do you?"

"At least she's not in jail." R.J. said dejectedly staring at the cement block wall.

"You're wrong there, R.J., she's in a bigger prison than you can imagine. The only two things that she loves in the whole world have been taken away from her. The saddest part is she didn't know how much she loved them, and now she can't get them back. And everywhere she goes people talk about her and stare at her and say what a terrible mother she is, and she can't deny it, because it's true. R.J. you were part of that nightmare, and so was Jimmy, and all of the hate, and anger, and running away isn't going to take you one inch farther from the problem or one inch closer to the solution. It's time that you and that drunk, as you call her, turn around and roll up your sleeves and start fighting to get out of the mess that you're in. R.J., all of the self loathing, and self pity won't get you anywhere. You may not know it, but there are a lot of good people trying the best they can to get you out of here and on the right track, and there are hundreds and maybe thousands of good people praying for your kid brother to wake up and be the happy little teenage boy he deserves to be. Do you understand what I'm saying?"

"I don't know. I just don't know," R.J. whimpered, shaking his head.

"R.J., I want to give you something you've never had before. I want to give you a God you can count on, and believe in, and pray to. Now come over here and pray with me."

"What good will that do?" R.J. resisted.

"What harm will it do?" Johnny shot back. "You tell me who you're praying to, who you're asking for help from, who's giving you comfort on this crappy night, and we'll both pray to that person, and see what it does for us."

R.J. sat quietly kicking the leg of his bed with his head hung down. "Just go away. There's no hope for me," he said.

"R.J.!" Johnny said pleading through the bars to the distraught broken soul in the corner,

"I want more than anything in the whole world to help you find peace and to get you out of this mess you're in. Please, come over here and pray with me."

R.J. meekly got up from his bunk and slowly walked to Johnny, and for the first time in his adult life put his trust in another human being. They both hugged each other through the bars, and Johnny prayed:

> *"Father, lift this young man up. He is yours. He begs your forgiveness and asks for the opportunity to do your will. Together, Father as a brother and a friend we ask for a miracle to bring Jimmy back to us that we may all learn to serve you Lord. Amen."*

R.J. was weakened and went back and sat on his bed. He was embarrassed and in a place where he had never been before.

Johnny said, "R.J. a prayer is just a personal talk with the best friend you have ever had. Tell Him what you think. Tell Him what you feel. Get rid of all of your doubts and fears, because from now on He will be the best thing that ever happened to your whole family. I promise.

I'll see you tomorrow and we'll begin to make life better for the Hackalas. Good night and God bless you my brother."

CHAPTER 15

"Johnny get out here before it falls," yelled Helen from the hallway. "It'll be ruined if you don't hurry."

"Is he coming?" hollered Jenny from the kitchen.

"I don't know why a grown man wants to spend his whole life laying in bed. Johnny are you up yet?"

"Yes I'm up. Thank you very much for caring so much about my rest. What in the world is going on around here?" Johnny asked pulling on his bathrobe and throwing open the door.

"Is there a fire? Did the world come to an end? What?" He said throwing his hands in the air.

"It's Pannukakku." Helen and Jenny both shouted at the same time, laughing and clapping hands.

Johnny looked at both of them as if they had lost their minds. "Pahnu- what?"

"Pannukakku, Finnish Oven Pancakes, silly," said Jenny as she gave him a hug.

"And if you don't eat them when they first come out of the oven," said Helen.

"They fall," said Jenny, "and that's why we have to hurry into the kitchen right now."

The two ladies pushed Johnny up to the stove to see the cast iron skillet over flowing with the rich pan cakey, eggy treat, which was starting to deflate right before their eyes.

"Quick," directed Helen. "plates." The oozing treat was slid from the pan onto warmed plates and covered with butter and Thimbleberry jam. The three gourmets sat down and giggled like little children as they savored the rare treat.

"When I was a little girl," Helen said, "my mother would get up extra early on Sunday morning and build a wood fire in the kitchen stove. We lived outside of Chassell. Mother would go out to the hen house for fresh eggs, and when the kitchen was warm and the fire in the stove was really hot, she would wake up Dad, and my brothers and I. By the time we were all dressed, mother had stirred the eggs into the fresh cream and flour. The secret was to beat it until it was thick and creamy then pour it into buttered skillets and slide it into the oven. Dad would heat the maple syrup from our own sugar bush, and the whole family would all sit down to have breakfast before going to Mass. It just sort of set the tone for the entire day and made us all grateful for what we had and who we were. One by one, the boys all grew up and married and moved on and I finally met Arvin and moved up here to Hancock. I always think of the old days when I make Pannukakku," she mused.

"It's important to enjoy every day God gives you and try to make it special," Helen said to both of us. "You two are so full of life and have so much to live for. I pray for you both every night, because I know God has a plan for our little community, and we're all part of it," she said as she carried the empty plates to the sink.

"What are you doing in here?" asked Gretta from the nurses station.

"Please don't tell on me, I'll lose my job," said a startled Miia.

"Who are you?" Gretta asked, noticing Miia's work uniform.

"I'm a friend of Jimmy's, I work here. Please let me go."

"I've never seen you before. Where do you work?"

"I work in housekeeping, but I know Jimmy from before. I know R.J.," she said, already sorry she had mentioned the older brother's name.

"Well, if you leave right now, I won't tell anyone. Okay?" Gretta didn't need any more hassles than she already had.

"Thank you," Miia said starting to leave, "but" she hesitated, "I think I saw his eyes flutter."

"You what?"

"Just before you came in, Jimmy's eyes opened a little." Miia said.

Gretta hurried to Jimmy's bedside and leaned over the young boy. "I think you're right," she said. "Quick, go back to work; I'm going to call the doctor."

Ten minutes later Doctor Sinjay was leaning over Jimmy with his penlight creating what was obviously some discomfort to Jimmy. "The situation is changing, but at this point all we can do is monitor his vitals and see what happens. We know his brain functions should be there, but may be diminished. Put someone in here to watch him and if there are any changes, call me immediately."

Jimmy seemed to be having a war inside his brain. His head would toss and turn, and his eyes would flutter, but he never quite woke up from what was going on inside. The nurse's aide sat quietly reading a book, as the night turned to day.

Johnny tapped on the window of Berg Insurance Agency at 9:00 am but the door was locked and there was no light on inside. Johnny looked through the window at the dark office and checked his watch again and wondered if maybe Howard had a morning appointment, or had overslept. He decided to drive up the block to Howard's house and noticed his car still in the driveway. It was obvious that with fresh snow on the steps Howard hadn't been out yet, so he pulled up behind his car, got out and rapped on the side door. No answer. Johnny pulled out his phone and called. No answer. Johnny called Chief Tom Burley.

"Hancock P.D. May I help you," responded the desk officer.

"This is Johnny Hendricks, is Chief Burley in."

"I'll connect," replied the desk.

"Good morning Johnny, is this a social call?" asked the Chief.

Johnny explained what had happened after the meeting last night with Howard and his inability to find him this morning. "I've got to confess Chief, I'm kind of concerned. He did mention some health problems, and I can't seem to get him to come to the door. I don't want to concern the whole neighborhood, but I think we should check in on him if that's possible. I guess Maggie's not there this morning, so what do you think?" Johnny asked.

"I'll be right over," said Burley.

The chief pulled in behind Johnny and met him at the side door. After rapping on the glass and jiggling the handle, he strategically placed his knee and shoulder against the door and using his body weight forced his way into the rear hallway.

"Howard it's Tom Burley, are you here?" He asked. "You stay here," he said to Johnny.

"Howard its Tom Burley from the Police Department. Are you okay?" Tom pulled out his flash light and walked through the living room up the stairs to the bed rooms. Tom opened a bed room door and there was Howard unconscious twisted in a blood soaked sheet.

"Barbara, this is Tom Burley," he said into his two-way. "I'm at 1214 Brock Street in Terrace Park. It's Howard Berg. He's unconscious in bed and passing blood. We need an ambulance ASAP." Tom ran back down the stairs, told Johnny what was happening and to move the cars into the street. Tom ran back up stairs to help Howard as Johnny guided the ambulance up the driveway. Ten minutes later, Howard was carried out of the house strapped to a gurney with oxygen in his nose and a confused look on his face. With Tom leading the ambulance toward Portage Health, Johnny wondered what could possibly happen next.

Johnny tried Kitty's phone number hoping to find Maggie.

"Hello," said Maggie. "Kitty's sleeping right now."

"Maggie, this is Johnny Hendricks. I am at your house and Howard has had a medical emergency. An ambulance has taken him up to Portage Health. He is passing blood, but he is conscious and the EMS has everything under control." There was silence on the other end of the line. "Maggie, are you there?"

"Is he…"

"I don't know anything else; I can be at Kitty's in five minutes and pick you up. Be out in front." Johnny hung up his phone and jumped in his van. Johnny drove right up to the side emergency doors of the hospital and Maggie jumped out of the van without even closing the door. As she ran through admittance, she grabbed the first person dressed in scrubs and shouted, "I'm Maggie Hackala, where is my husband?"

"Come over and sit down, Mrs. Hackala. Howard's in good hands. We need you to give us some information so that we can help him."

"Can I see him?" Maggie asked, looking around as if she were being held captive.

"In just a few minutes, please, we are stabilizing him, and we really need you to help us now, okay?" the nurse insisted.

Maggie was lost as Johnny took the clipboard and helped her to find her insurance cards. With the essentials completed, they took Maggie back to the lay in where Howard was cleaned up and resting in an ill fitting hospital gown with I.V. needles stuck in both arms. When the nurse pulled the curtain back, Howard and Maggie both looked at each other and started crying. Maggie rushed forward and hugged Howard and kissed him on the lips. It was something they hadn't done in ten years. Johnny closed the curtain and headed for his van.

It was close to noon when Johnny pulled back into the downtown area and decided he'd better go tell Kitty where her sister was and what had happened to Howard. Kitty was sitting on the couch drinking a cup of tea in her old sweats when Johnny knocked on the door. She looked out through the curtains and was glad to see him.

"You missed all the excitement," Johnny said as she invited him in.

"What happened?" she asked, flopping back down on the couch.

Johnny told her about finding Howard and picking up Maggie and what was going on up at the hospital.

"I told him a long time ago that if he didn't stop yelling at everybody he was going to blow a gasket," Kitty said. "Is he going to be all right?"

"I think he may be laid up for awhile, but he's going to have to ease up and learn to take better care of himself."

"Fat chance of that," Kitty shot back. "He's been a walking heart attack ever since he and Maggie started dating. He just can't help himself."

"You know, with everything that's happening, your whole family is going to have to step back and take a look at what you're doing and how you're treating each other. None of you can continue to live like this, Kitty. If we're lucky enough to get your two boys back home and healthy, things have got to change, and that starts with you. I'm not here to lecture you. You're a grown woman, but I think we're going to have to lean on the Lord a little to get things straightened out."

"Well, I don't know, but I trust you Pastor, and I sure am grateful for the help."

"What you need right now is a cheeseburger down at Rudy's. Let's go down and tell him what's going on," Johnny said. "I got some one I'd like you to meet who wants to talk to you."

"How ya doin kids?" said Rudy, as Johnny and Kitty walked in the door.

"Fine boss," said Kitty. "I want to introduce you to my new Pastor, Johnny Hendricks. He's not really a preacher, but he's helped me out so much with Jimmy and R.J., that I feel like he's my own personal pastor, and I hope he doesn't mind."

"It's a privilege to meet you," said Johnny extending his hand across the bar.

"Same here," said Rudy. "You're all she talks about lately," he laughed.

"Rudy, I know Johnny doesn't drink, but how about a couple of cheeseburgers and cokes. We're really hungry."

"Comin right up," Rudy said and headed for the grill.

Rudy brought the cokes, and Johnny and Kitty went over to a corner booth.

"Who was it you wanted me to meet?" Kitty asked, sipping on her soda.

"Well, first I've got to tell you a story and it concerns R.J. Then I've got to tell you another story and it concerns Jimmy. Then, I want to introduce you to a friend of yours that you haven't met yet, okay?"

"It sounds crazy, but okay."

Johnny told Kitty how he had met Miia, and what she had told him, and when they had finished their burgers, he ordered two more cokes, and went down the back hall of the bar to get Miia.

"Yah know, you look familiar," Kitty said as Miia followed Johnny up to the booth.

"Hi, my name's Miia Virtinen, and I feel like I've known you for a long time."

Johnny smiled at Kitty and said, "Let's sit down, Miia, and get acquainted."

Rudy brought over three colas, cleaned off the empty plates, winked at Miia and went back behind the bar.

It took most of the afternoon for Miia to tell Kitty about her relationships with both of her sons. Kitty was angry, then sad, then dumbfounded and finally grateful for all she was learning about her two sons.

"Miia, I must have been blind all these years. When Jimmy disappeared, the police asked me who his friends were. I really couldn't think of one person in his life, and I was so embarrassed. What a terrible mother I've been." Kitty started weeping into a paper napkin and put her head on the table. Miia put her arm around her and comforted her.

"And who was there for you?" Miia said, handing her another napkin. "Who decided you had to be the tough one and raise two boys all by yourself with a drunken bully for and ex- husband?"

"Who told you that?" Kitty asked sniffling.

"Jimmy." Miia said. "Don't you think those boys knew what you were going through? My father was the same mean drunk as your husband, and my mother not only got herself beat up, but she got me and my brother beat up, too. My brother finally got big enough to beat the old man up and got out of the house. He joined the Army, but before he left he told dad that if he ever laid another hand on me again, he'd come back and kill him. My mother is still there. You at least had the courage to throw the bum out and protect your kids. They know that. They just didn't know how to help you." Kitty stared at the table.

"Honey," Kitty said softly. "I've never had a real friend or a daughter, but if I could have either it would be you. You are very special to me and my kids. You are welcome in my home anytime. Johnny, everything you do for me makes my life better. Thank you."

"Why don't the three of us go up to Portage Health and visit that rascal right now."

The three friends said goodbye to Rudy and left the bar laughing on their way to Johnny's van.

"I'm glad to see you," said Dr. Marong as Kitty and her friends entered Jimmy's room. Look, come and see." The Doctor shined his pen light into Jimmy's fluttering eyes. His body began to react and he began making sounds. "This is indeed very encouraging. The nurse last night noticed the eyes fluttering." Miia smiled. "Then this morning there was more movement in the limbs. I am optimistic. We must wait and see, but these are all good signs. Now that you are here, I will finish my rounds. Excuse me," and the doctor left.

"I think this is a good time for a celebration," Johnny said. "Kitty, Miia, Why don't you both take one of Jimmy's hands." He then reached out to both of the women and prayed,

*"Almighty God, we feel our young brother stirring
and we know that his life is in your hands. We
are very grateful that he is even alive, but if it is
your will to bring him back to us, to You we give
all the praise and glory. Amen."*

Kitty squeezed Johnny and Jimmy's hands, and they both squeezed back. Kitty quickly dropped Johnny's hand and took Jimmy's hand in both of hers, and his fingers grabbed her thumb. Kitty began massaging Jimmy's arms and hands and his body began to react. Tears began running down Kitty's face and she began trembling, whispering "It's Mommy, it's Mommy, wake up Jimmy, its Mommy." Jimmy tried to rise but was too weak, and began to thrash around the bed. Johnny pressed the nurses light, and in minutes the room was filed with specialists. Kitty, Johnny and Miia were led into the hallway. Dr. Marong explained that Jimmy's body had been inert for so long that this specially trained team was called to work on his bones and muscles to make sure that he didn't hurt himself. The head of the coma triage team came into the hallway thirty minutes later and said, "Let's go down to my office."

"I'm Dr. Schultz," he said when they arrived, "Please have a seat."

"I'm Jimmy's mother, Kitty. Is he all right? Why can't I see him?"

"Kitty, the word "alright" is not a medical term, and in these cases doesn't mean much. Physically I'd say with some physical therapy he'll come back nicely. He's a strong young teenager. Mentally, we don't know. We don't know what his mental state was when he ran into that bus and we don't know where it is now. I can tell you this much, he seems to be babbling something about R.J. I think that's his brother but, any kind of emotion might set him back. We'll keep him quiet, and let him acclimate and see what happens. I know this is very hard on you, but on the bright side I think it's safe to say our young man is trying to get back. So let him rest, and as soon as there are any changes you will be the first to know."

"Let's go tell Maggie and see how Howard is doing," said Kitty.

As they passed the hospital chapel, Kitty stopped, opened the door and slowly walked to the cross in the front. As she lowered herself down on her knees in front of the symbol of her brand-new God she prayed. For the first time, she was no longer using Johnny's God. She had her own.

Johnny and Miia stood outside of the stained glass chapel, and with tears running down his face, he called his Mom and Dad to tell them about a couple of miracles that had happened.

It was no great revelation that everything happened in God's time, but as usual the confirmation and joy of living in His world gave Johnny peace. Kitty came out of the chapel with a glow on her face and together the three went upstairs to see Howard.

CHAPTER 16

"What are we going to do now that Howard's in the hospital?" asked Father Walter on Saturday morning as he, Johnny and Bob Heikinen sat around the table at Kaleva's.

"Well, the doctors said the meeting on Tuesday is off the table, as well as the rest of his schedule for the next couple of weeks. Doctor Burns said Howard's body is a disaster. It's a wonder he survived that exploding ulcer."

Bob and Walter shook their heads in agreement.

"Maggie said she's taking him home, locking the doors and turning off the telephones." Johnny said. "She means business."

"It looks like you're in the driver's seat on Tuesday Johnny. Who do you want to take with you?" Bob asked, taking a sip of coffee.

"You know, I've kind of been praying on this all night and I've got to talk to a few people, but I think I might have a plan. I'll call everybody as soon as I can put it together and we'll see if it makes any sense."

The three men finished their breakfast and walked out of the coffee shop into a brisk November breeze to face the day. Johnny called Kitty from his car.

"Any news?" he asked.

"They say he's about the same. He's taken a few fluids and asked about R.J. but he's not really talking. It's like he's got a secret." Kitty said.

"Have they said anything about visiting him?" Johnny asked.

"They said they would call soon," she responded.

"I've got some business this morning. Maybe we can try and go up and see him this afternoon. I'll call you."

"Thank you Johnny. Goodbye."

Johnny pulled up in front of the Houghton Court House, parked his car and called his dad to explain what he had in mind. As he walked into the Sheriff's lock-up, Ron Burch was on desk duty once again.

"How ya doin Johnny?" said Ron as if they were old pals.

"Ronny, nice to see you again," Johnny shot back. "How's the wife?"

"Great, she was really impressed when I told her that we had met."

"You tell her that we'll be looking for her when we get the community work projects up and going," Johnny said."

"I'll tell her, Johnny," he said.

"Ron, I wonder if you could help me. I need to talk to R.J. and it concern's something personal. Would it be possible to go into his cell for a few minutes so we won't have to shout at each other?"

"I don't see why not. It'll be a regular pastoral visit. Let me get the key."

Ron led Johnny into the lock-up. "Wake up R.J. you've got company. Your preacher's come for a visit."

When Officer Burch locked them both in, and left, Johnny sat down next to R.J. and said, "How are you holding up?"

"How do you think," R.J. said.

"Well," Johnny said with a smile, "I've got some good news, and some great news. Which do you want first?"

"What?" R.J. said.

"I take it that's the great news. Your brother's awake."

R.J. jumped up and down a couple of times and started laughing. "When?"

"Well, it started a little bit yesterday and today he seems to be fully conscious. But, he's confused and hasn't said anything to anyone except that he wants to talk to you."

"I need to talk to him now," R.J. shouted.

"Now R.J., I want you to sit down and listen to me, and I want you to trust me, okay. Jimmy's not out of the woods, yet. His body needs physical therapy, and he's still not completely alert. The doctors are afraid that any excitement might send him back into a coma. Do you understand? Now, I'm guessing that when he disappeared and ended up at Victor's Junk Yard, you had something to do with that. Am I right?"

R.J. shook his head.

"I'm also guessing that when Jimmy escaped, he was trying to find you. Am I right?"

Once again R.J. nodded to Johnny.

"I think that we need to call the Sheriff and tell him the whole truth and then see if they will take you to see your brother's doctors and try and help Jimmy. Are you willing to do that?"

Johnny shouted for Ron, and told him to call the County Sheriff and Chief Burley, and tell them to come to the jail immediately.

Johnny said, "I'll be staying here. We still have some things to discuss."

It was late Saturday afternoon before the squad cars pulled up in front of Portage Health, and the two senior police officers followed by two deputies on either side of R.J. entered the hospital. Johnny pulled up five minutes later with Kitty. The meeting was held in the Doctor's lounge, and the ground rules were laid out as to what could be said by R.J. to his brother. A full confession was made and signed in R.J.'s jail cell, so no new evidence could be made available.

Johnny and Kitty waited in the hallway with nothing to do but pray.

When the doctors led the police out of the room, R.J. saw his mother, and said, "I'm sorry. I'm going to make this right," and walked between his guards down to Jimmy's room.

The lights in the room were dimmed and the nurse's aide sat quietly as Jimmy lay with his eyes closed. Only the doctor, one guard, and R.J. were allowed in the room, and no one made a sound. The police officer stood by the door. Dr. Marong took Jimmy's pulse, and he began to stir. R.J. went to the other side of the bed and took Jimmy's other hand.

"I didn't tell," he whispered to his older brother and smiled. R.J. brushed back Jimmy's hair and said, "It's alright now Jimmy. Everything's fine. You just need to get better. Everything's going to be better from now on. I promise."

Jimmy took both of his hands and tried to pull R.J. into bed with him.

"Bring my mother in please," R.J. said to the guard. The door opened and Kitty rushed in and stood next to R.J. "Jimmy I can't stay right now, but I'll be back soon and then we'll all be together," R.J. said. He squeezed Jimmy's hand, smiled at Kitty and walked out the door.

Johnny went down to the lobby, bought a soda and called his folks. He was exhausted after all of the events of the day and just needed a hug from home.

"Hi Dad," Johnny said. "How are things going down in the sane part of the world?"

"Hi son, I guess you are still up to your elbows in Yooper mayhem, eh."

"If you've got a few minutes I'll try and get you caught up. Things are changing so quickly around here that I'm not even sure where I fit into this picture anymore. You know, I came up here to relax and run a pool hall for kids, but now it seems like I'm in charge of everybody and everything. I've got Howard in the hospital with a bleeding ulcer. I've got Jimmy coming out of his coma. The town council and the police force are counting on me to make everything right and if that's not enough, I've got to go down to Gaylord on Tuesday without Howard and represent the whole Keweenaw Peninsula and try to get the State of Michigan to help us free R.J., who incidentally is turning out to be a pretty nice young man. If it sounds like I'm ranting a little bit, I guess I am," said Johnny sounding like a leaky tire running out of air. After a quiet moment, he said, "Thanks for listening Dad, I needed that."

"How's Jenny?" Dad asked.

"You know dad, it seems like I haven't seen her in days." Johnny said

"That would be my next call, son. But first, is Father Walter the head of the Clergy Association that's backing you?"

"Yes, why do you ask?"

"I've got an idea I want to run by him, and If it makes sense to him, I'll have him give you a call and you two can work it out. We'll talk about it later. In the mean time you'd better take those two ladies of yours to church tomorrow morning. I don't think it will do you any harm. Who knows, maybe God will see fit to help you a little? Goodbye son."

Johnny smiled at his dad's sense of humor and realized how insignificant his problems were. After all, everything that he had complained about was being taken care of by God and all he had to do was follow his heart. *"Lord, forgive me for thinking that this world can't run without me. Sometimes I can be so stupid,"* he thought.

Kitty came into the lobby, took his arm and said that Jimmy said hello. As they walked out to the van, they were both smiling.

"Hi Jenny," he said, relieved to hear her voice.

"To whom am I speaking?" Jenny asked.

"Come on Jenny, it hasn't been that long, has it?"

"Is this Bruce?"

"Jenny, I'm parked out in front of your house and I'm dying to see you."

"Barney?" She offered

"Jenny if you don't come out right now, I'm going to break your door down."

"Well, aren't we the aggressive one, Mr. Hendricks. Give me a second to get my coat."

Jenny ran out the front door, climbed into the van, and gave Johnny their first serious kiss sense they had met.

"Wow," he said. "Why don't you go back out and do that again."

"Why waste the trip," she replied and they kissed again, and suddenly all of Johnny's worries and anxieties flew out the window.

"Now I've got to be at the radio station in two hours, so let's go up town and get a burger and fries and celebrate our new getting back together. Okay?"

Johnny dropped her off an hour later and said, "Don't forget our date for church tomorrow."

Johnny was lying in bed listening to his favorite D.J. when his phone rang.

"Johnny, this is Walt. Did I wake you up?"

"No, I was just sitting here listening to Jenny spinning C.D.'s on her radio show on WMTU."

"You're kidding. I didn't know she was a local celebrity. We'll have to take advantage of that and throw a little advertising her way. Anyway, the reason that I called was in response to a conversation I had with your Dad this afternoon. I don't mind saying that for a preacher, he's a real wheeler dealer."

"I've been told that on more than one occasion," Johnny replied.

"Anyway," Walt said, "he suggested that you take R.J. with you on Tuesday to Gaylord and show him off. Now, I know you're asking, how can we make that happen?" Walt paused for effect. "The answer is "The Shepherd Program." Are you familiar with how they work?"

"No, I've heard the name before, but…"

"Let me give you some examples," Walt said. "Different denominations use them for alcohol programs. Others use them for needy children, or like in our case abused children who have fallen through the cracks and need guidance and supervision to straighten out their lives. Sound familiar? Now, through the HHCA, I called around this evening and found out that Mel Simpson from the Community Presbyterian Church over in Houghton has a Shepherd's Program and we talked for a half an hour about a parishioner of his named Ernie Sugg. Now, you don't know Ernie, but he is kind of a local legend around here."

CHAPTER 17

Ernie Sugg

If there ever was a poster child for the Yooper of the year, Ernie Sugg would have been a candidate. He didn't have one of those great Finnish names with an "inen" or a vowel on the end, no it was just Sugg, plain and simple. And for forty some years, no one could ever remember anybody ever calling him Ernest either. It was always just good old Ernie Sugg. His dad Joe was what they called a tough bugger. He walked across Europe with General George "Blood and Guts" Patton and his 7th Army chasing Adolph and his German Army into oblivion. Then he came home and married Bea St. Andre and raised eight kids up on the hill in Houghton. Joe was always good with his hands, so he taught his oldest son George how to use a hammer and a saw. Together the two of them started up a family carpentry business. It was seventeen years later when Joe was almost forty that Ernie was born, and Bea died during child birth. Most of Joe's kids were grown and he didn't have room in his heart for the child he blamed for the loss of his wife, so Ernie's sixteen year old sister Bernice was left with the chore. Ernie was babied by everyone but Joe, and although Ernie never mentioned it, you could tell he felt like an outsider. Ernie was a natural athlete and being from Houghton, his dream was to play hockey for the Michigan Tech Huskies. The teams and the coaches were legendary and with eleven months of winter, and one month of bad ice, as people often joked, kids laced up the skates as soon as they could walk. Ernie played through high school and in the late eighties received a scholarship to play at Michigan Tech to help rejuvenate a sagging program.

Life changed for Ernie in his junior year when President George H.W. Bush declared war on Iraq, and Ernie felt the need to serve his country. He enlisted after his spring term. Kuwait had been seized by the Iraqis and the coalition forces were sent in to drive them out. Ernie's platoon followed a tank division into a fire fight, and shrapnel from an Iraqi shell took off his lower right leg below the knee. Two days later a cease fire was called and Ernie was on his way back to the States for a new leg and a new way of life.

The shell ruined more than his ability to walk normally, and it was only after he returned from Walter Reed to Houghton, and married his high school sweet heart Brenda, that they found out that he was unable to have children.

"We'll adopt," said Brenda.

"We'll talk about it," said Ernie, and so the dialogue began.

Brenda had nine brothers and sisters, and with Ernie's seven brothers and sisters it seemed there was not a night of the week that they were not babysitting or going to a school play or ball game.

Their lives changed one Sunday morning when they entered the Houghton Community Presbyterian Church, and sat in their usual pew next to Ben and Judy Baxter who were sitting on either side of two beautiful little African American girls.

"Good morning Ben," Ernie said, nodding at Judy. "I see you've got company."

"Brenda, Ernie, these are our new foster daughters, Kisha and Alizea." The girls with pretty new dresses and their hair done in corn rows smiled at the Suggs.

The pastor rose to the pulpit and the service began, but both Ernie and Brenda could hardly wait for coffee hour to find out what was going on.

"You know there are over ten thousand children in Michigan who need parents and we weren't ready to adopt," said Judy, "so we contacted the Foster Care Program. It was easy. These beautiful little girls have parents right here in Houghton who are going through some things and so they need some space. So, Ben and I are Kisha and Alizea's foster mom and dad."

The Suggs talked about it all the way home. The number of homeless children of all ages was staggering, so they prayed on it and the next week they went to a meeting. That was twenty years and countless kids ago.

Johnny dropped Helen and Jenny off after Mass, and then headed for Houghton to meet Ernie at the county lock up. The three men were escorted into the holding cell by the Sheriff, and R.J. rose from his bunk wondering what he had done now.

"Relax," said Johnny. "I want you to meet a couple of people who are here to help you, and of course I'm sure you remember the Sheriff."

"Gentlemen," the Sheriff said, "I'm going to leave now, but it's important that you know R.J." the Sheriff said looking him straight in the eye, "that in all my years of law enforcement I've never seen anything like this. If you're smart young man, you'll take advantage of it. Have a good day gentlemen."

The four stood quietly as the Sheriff left.

"R.J., My name is Ernie Sugg and I want to tell you who I am and what we have in mind."

Together the three men explained to R.J. why it was important that he accompany Johnny to Gaylord on Tuesday, not as a prisoner, but as part of Ernie's Shepherd Program and also because of his age, as a foster child living in Ernie's home. It would be similar to a parole program, but wouldn't go on his permanent record. He would also have an opportunity to learn a skilled trade in that Ernie was a licensed carpenter. Things were moving too fast for R.J., but the thought of finally getting out of this cell seemed like a dream.

"What about Jimmy and my mom?" he asked.

"When Jimmy is healthy enough he will go home, but you have to admit that there has to be some major changes in all of your lives to make this thing work. Somehow you've got to trust us R.J. Believe me we want nothing but the best for you," Johnny said.

"Guys, I don't think I've ever thanked anybody in my whole life and I'm not sure how to thank you now, but I promise I'll try and do whatever I can to make this right."

"That's good enough for us, R.J." said Ernie. Tomorrow we'll get a judge to legalize all this and get you out of here so we can start planning for Tuesday."

The two men both shook R.J.'s hand and walked out of the jail hopeful that they had covered all of the bases and that there wouldn't be any surprises before Tuesday. They would all have to meet with the rest of the council tomorrow evening for a final planning session so that they would be ready for what ever the State threw at them and hope for the best.

Johnny said goodbye, jumped in his van and called Jenny.

"Hello," she answered.

"This is Barney, have there been any calls for me?" Johnny asked.

"Quick, hang up, I'm expecting a call from my boyfriend," she quipped.

"Put your coat on. He's on his way."

Deer hunting season started the following weekend and so all of the law enforcement agencies involved with R.J. and his legal mess were eager to get it behind them so they could prepare for their biggest weekend of the fall season. Bob Heikinen and Tom Burley carried the legal football through the ins and outs of the court and penal system. By noon R.J. was standing in front of the courthouse wondering what was next. The judgment had been clear. R.J. would be in the custody of Johnny or Ernie every day at 8:00 am and returned to the lock up at 6:00 pm unless otherwise ordered. He was allowed to leave at 5:00 a.m. on Tuesday for a trip to Gaylord and return to his cell immediately afterwards. Otherwise he was not to leave the Houghton-Hancock area. In three weeks he would be re-evaluated for further considerations.

R.J. constantly fought the temptation to bend the rules for his own advantage. The scar on his arm was his best reminder of what could happen when he lied to others. Besides, he had this new secret friend that he confided with who he talked to every night and so far things were working out okay."

"I'm grateful you all could make it this evening and I hope that we won't have a reason to meet together again until after the holidays," Johnny said. "I have here a copy of the judgment handed down by Judge Tumi on R.J. and I think it's more than fair. You'll see in your copy that there will be a re-evaluation after three weeks. Sitting next to me is a new friend of mine. If you don't know him, his name is Ernie Sugg, and if this world had more people like he and his wife Brenda, we would have less R.J.'s. Anyway," Johnny said smiling, "Ernie will explain phase two."

"Hi everybody, as Johnny said, "I'm Ernie, and with my wife Brenda we are the middle men, or I should say the middle people. Brenda and I both grew up here in Houghton, came from big families and hoped to raise one of our own. Years ago an Iraqi shell put an end to that dream. We considered adoption, but then realized the world was already full of loving children who needed ready-made parents to love them and show them the way. I was never much of a Christian before I was lying on that table at Walter Reed, but in looking down the hallway at a bunch of blown up heroes I was humbled by who I was on this planet. So," he sighed, "Bren and I went to a foster care meeting, and dat was dat. I can't tell you how many kids we've shuffled through that old house of ours, but we get a lot more Christmas cards than anybody else I know." He paused. "With the judge's okay, and believe me when I say we are good friends of this judge, we will move R.J. into our home and make a first rate carpenter and citizen out of him. You have my word. You betcha."

There wasn't a dry eye in the room. Ernie sat down and Johnny hugged him.

"Any questions?" Johnny asked. 'Let's join hands and pray for our success tomorrow."

> *"Father God we thank you for Ernie and Brenda, and all these fine people here who are trying to make this world a better place to live. Please, grant R.J. and myself travel mercies tomorrow on our trip to Gaylord and allow the State representatives to see the justice in what we are trying to do. Amen."*

"Drive safely going home tonight and I'll give you a full report on Wednesday morning."

Everyone filed out of the commission room shaking hands with Ernie and thanking him for his service.

CHAPTER 18

Helen made a basket full of ham and egg sandwiches, two Thermos' of coffee and a sliced Povititsa wrapped in waxed paper.

"You be careful now," she said. "The bucks are rutting and they'll be running back and forth across the highways all the way down." she said.

"We'll be careful, now you go back to bed and thank you, Helen."

"You're very welcome Johnny," she said, and gave him a big hug.

R.J. and Officer Danny were sitting in a cruiser with the motor running when Johnny pulled up. Danny flashed his lights as R.J. ran for the van.

"Gonna be a long ride," Johnny said. "About seven hours I figure."

"Better than seven hours sittin on yer bunk starin at the wall," said R.J.

They drove along through the dark with the radio stations fading, so Johnny turned it off.

"There's a basket of sandwiches and a couple of jugs of coffee behind your seat if you can reach them," Johnny said.

R.J. opened the basket, pulled out two aluminum foil wrappers and handed one to Johnny. He then took a thermos, poured a coffee and put it in Johnny's cup holder, and did the same for himself. When the smell of hot coffee and warm ham and egg sandwiches filled the van, life suddenly got a lot better.

"So where'd you grow up?" asked Johnny through a mouthful of sandwich losing part of it down the front of his jacket.

"Laurium," said R.J. not offering anything else.

"I've been to Laurium," said Johnny. Tony's pasties, right?"

"There's a lot more to Laurium than Tony's pasties."

"Like what?" Johnny challenged.

R.J. sat quietly for a moment. "There used to be a real city there. Now it's just a ghost town. Calumet's the same way; Mohawk; all a dem. There's nobody here anymore."

"Where'd they go?" Johnny asked

"Man, where does anybody go? They just up and leave. There's nothing to do here. This time of year my dad used to wait for the snow so he could shovel off roofs. Can you imagine having that to look forward to? When I was a kid they would be out poachin deer. They probably still are today. He'd come home smellin like deer guts, whisky and cigarettes. That's what I wanted to be when I grew up, but he didn't want me. He didn't want any of us. Just because of my mother. She was the one that ruined it all for everybody. If only she could have left him alone he might have stayed and then everything would have been all right. But no, she always had to have everything her own way and look how we all ended up."

They drove down into the Seney Flats and the sun started rising from the east.

"What does yer dad do?" R.J. asked out of the blue.

"You know, a better question might be, what did my dad do when I was a kid? And the answer is he used to make soup. He also worked in a gas station. He used to drive truck and he used to sing on the streets of Grand Rapids with my mother."

"Why did he do that?" R.J. asked.

"So he could get drunks to come in and eat his soup."

"It must have been pretty bad soup," R.J. and Johnny laughed.

"Well, it didn't have any tasty venison in it, but it was nutritious and it did sober up the men and women to listen to my dad preach the Word."

"And what word was that?" R.J. asked

"The word of God."

"I should have known."

"Yes you should have," Johnny said and they both laughed again.

"So that's how you got all holy, I guess." R.J. said.

"No, nobody was all holy back then. We were too busy. Mom was a Mexican immigrant. She wasn't lucky enough to be born in America like you and me, so she always ran the risk of being deported. Back then she took all the jobs that no one else would do because she was illegal. At night she went to school to learn English and study to be an American. She was a busy lady. She and dad started with nothing just like your folks.

"Yeah, but it was different." R.J. said.

"In what way?" Johnny asked.

"I don't know. It sounds like they liked each other. Not like my folks."

"Your folks loved each other, R.J. or they wouldn't have had you and Jimmy," Johnny said. "You've got to believe that," he emphasized. "Remember they were together for a long time. But sometimes people hit a rough patch and things don't go so well, and they don't know who to turn to for help. In their case, your grandparents tried to help, but they weren't enough. So things never got a chance to get better. I'm not saying that God is the only way, but if they could have used Him like you and I did to work through some tricky situations, maybe we wouldn't be drinking the cold coffee right now. What do you think?"

"You sure do put a lot of stock in this God of yours," R.J. said.

"That's not true R.J., I put all my stock in Him and I deal with whatever life brings. Does that make any sense?"

"You're hard to argue with," R.J. said as they pulled into Newberry for gas. The trip to St. Ignace was uneventful with the exception of one lone white tail deer crossing the road south of Trout Lake.

R.J. had never seen the Big Mac Bridge before and was impressed as one of the last ore carriers of the year wended its way south towards Detroit. Johnny paid the $4.00 toll and kept his speed right at 45 miles per hour as strong winds buffeted the bridge from the west.

"Well, we're only an hour out of Gaylord, R.J. and then we'll see what the Governor has to throw at us," Johnny said.

"Are you really concerned?" R.J. asked.

"No, it's all in God's hands, whatever He decides we'll live with."

Johnny exited I-75 and made a left on to Main Street and pulled into a Burger King. They still had an hour before the meeting, and a Whopper and fries wouldn't do them any harm. Johnny asked the girl behind the counter where the County Court House was and she said it was down the block.

Johnny and R. J. entered the building right at 1:00 and told the Information desk that they had an appointment.

"Room 107," she replied, and the two men walked down the hallway.

"Good afternoon," said a man sitting behind a desk in a small office. Seated next to him was John Hendricks, Johnny's father.

"Good afternoon sir," greeted Johnny. R.J. nodded as they moved slowly towards the desk.

"My name is Alan Van den Elst and this is John Hendricks, who at least one of you may know."

"How do you do Mr. Van den Elst," Johnny said shaking his hand, "and how are you Dad. I'd like you both to meet R.J. Hackala, a Christian brother of mine and also the reason we are meeting today. Dad, what are you doing here?" Johnny asked.

"We'll get to all of that in a moment, but first have a seat. How was your trip?" Alan asked, as they all relaxed. "R.J., why don't you tell me?"

"It was okay I guess. I've never been this far south before. What are you going to do to me?" R.J. blurted out all at once.

"What should we do to you R.J.?" Alan asked. "Why are you here?" Van den Elst stared at him like the Grand Inquisitor at a medieval heresy trial.

"I messed up," R.J. paused, "Sir."

"That doesn't tell me much. You want me to help you, right. Tell me what you did to mess up."

R.J. looked around the room, and then at Johnny. "Well, I done a lotta things."

"I'm listening," said Alan.

John Hendricks sat quietly staring at his son.

"I don't know where to start," whimpered R.J. quietly.

"Let me help you," said Alan. "I have here a list of the convictions that you have had in Houghton County in your young lifetime. This list also includes everything that you stole. I'm sure that there were many times you didn't get caught, so this is what I want you to do. I want you and your friend Johnny to go into the next office and try to remember, as best you can, all of the other heists that you were so proud of. If you really want to stay out of prison, we are going to have to find a way to pay all of these people back. Do you understand R.J.? Do you agree to these conditions?"

"Yes sir. Just give me a chance," R.J. said, looking Van den Elst in the eyes.

"Mr. Hendricks and I will be waiting." Alan said.

The two young men took the pad of paper and quietly left the room.

"I want to thank you for giving this a chance to work, Alan," John said. "We are blessed to be working with Ernie Sugg and his program up in Houghton. We were also lucky to get Judge Tuvi to work with us as well. Now all we have to do is count on a kid who never got a fair shake in his whole life to trust a bunch of people who have never lifted a finger to help him before. Pretty large order, huh."

"Stranger things have happened," Alan said.

An hour later, Johnny and R.J. knocked on the door and came back into Room 107.

"That didn't take long," Alan said. "I guess you're not Jesse James after all."

"It wasn't easy, and I'm sure there are some I've missed, but if I remember them I will make amends I promise," R.J. said.

"I trust you," Alan said. "It looks like you've got your hands full right here, though. So R.J., I want you to stand in front of my desk and raise your right hand. Repeat after me: I promise to do my best to repay everyone on this list who I have wronged and to apologize for wrong doing."

R.J. did exactly that and sat down.

"Now this whole matter will be handled through Judge Tuvi's court room and he will release you upon your completion of this task. Until that time you will spend your nights in jail and will be on a work release program with Mr. Sugg teaching you the carpentry trade. Upon release from Judge Tuvi you will enter the foster care program living in Mr. Sugg's home as part of his family. Do you agree to these conditions R.J.?" Van den Elst asked.

"Mr. Van den Elst, Mr.Hendricks, Johnny, I just don't know what to say," R.J. said.

"You'd better say yes young man," Alan said, "or I'll take you over my knee."

Everyone laughed and hugged and R.J. wiped the tears from his eyes and promised them all he wouldn't let them down. He finally got a chance to formally meet John Senior and John told R.J. that he was looking forward to seeing more of him up in the Keweenaw. They all had long trips ahead of them, so they parted ways in front of the old court house and headed for I-75 to begin their long treks home.

Johnny and R.J. rode in silence, each one thinking about the events of the day and wondering how the future would unfold.

"You know Johnny," R.J. said in the darkness of the van as they once again crossed the Seney flats, "you're lucky to have such a great Dad."

"You are too," Johnny replied, keeping a sharp watch for deer crossing the highway.

"How do you figure that?" R.J. asked. "My Dad's a bum. He's a drunk that nobody respects. He'll never amount to nuthin."

"He raised you and Jimmy didn't he?" Johnny said. "He saw that you got fed and put clothes on your back through some pretty rough times I imagine."

"Well that was his job," R.J. said.

"You'd be surprised how many men with kids in this country aren't doing their job."

"Yeah but he deserted us," R.J. fought back.

"Did he desert you or did your mom throw him out and tell him not to come back," Johnny said patiently. Now that you're becoming an adult it's time you started looking at things from different perspectives. In your mom and dads case, maybe it was better for everyone for them to live separately. I'm sure it was more pleasant around the house without all that screaming and shouting."

"Yeah, but me and Jimmy missed Dad," R.J. said before he even realized what he said.

"We'll, now that you'll be on your own, maybe you'll have a chance to get to know him again." Johnny said.

"I doubt it," R.J. said. "He's always too busy to visit us."

Three hours later, Johnny pulled up in front of the Court House and Johnny took R.J. into the Jail. Danny Johnson was leaning on the counter and asked how it went.

"Well, Danny," Johnny said, "R.J. here is officially just a part time resident now, so we'll need a little more respect than usual."

"That goes both ways," said Danny as he shook hands with R.J. and led him back to the lock up.

CHAPTER 19

Ernie was at the jail at 8:00 am sharp and R.J. was waiting.

"Good morning Ron," Ernie said. "Did you feed this guy yet?"

"Yeah Ernie, he's good till lunch time," Officer Burch said.

"Well I'll try and bring him back as good as I found him," Ernie joked as they went out the front door to his Ford F250 heavy duty pick-up.

"R.J., most of the work I got this time of year is holding these student apartments together until Christmas break. So, this morning we've got some outside steps to nail together before we get hit with some serious snow. Now I know you know what serious snow is 'cause you're a Yooper born and raised, am I right?" Ernie asked slapping R.J. on the knee so hard that R.J. thought it might be broken.

"You betcha, Ernie," R.J. laughed. Then they both laughed as they drove straight up Houghton hill.

Ernie pulled an old torn and stained Carhart work coat and bib overalls out of the tool case in the truck bed and said, "Try these on for size." R.J. stood in the middle of the road, slid on the bibs and felt like he finally belonged to something.

"Whadaya tink?" R.J. asked taking a bow in his almost new ensemble.

"I tink I'll make a carpenter out of you yet, boyka," Ernie kidded back.

Together they walked around the hundred year old three-story one-time mansion. The grand residence of a mining superintendent had been converted into five separate apartments for students at Michigan Tech with entrances through the front and rear doors, as well as wooden fire escapes for the second and third floors. These exterior stair cases had to be inspected and repaired often to meet safety regulations for home owner's fire insurance. Ernie had many of these contracts in Houghton as well as in Hancock with Finlandia University student home owners. R.J. was quick to learn and didn't stand back when it was time to load and carry materials to the job sites.

Lunch time came around and Ernie took R.J. to the Hill Top Diner up on Sharon Avenue.

"What's up Sherri," said Ernie as he and R.J. walked through the front door of the busy diner.

"You just missed the rush, Boss. The troops are heading back to their one o clocks so I think I can squeeze you in."

"What's this Boss business?" R. J. asked Ernie as they found a table.

"Oh, this is another one of my side lines. When some of my daughters were growing up they couldn't find part time jobs while they were going to school so I bought the place and put them all to work. Now they're all grown up, so I hired Sherri. We close up at 7:00 p.m. So, it's just kind of for the students who don't have much money. They can get a burger and fries and it won't break the bank."

"Hi Boss." Sherri came over with menus. "Who's the new movie star with ya?" Sherri winked at R.J.

Sherri Bonzak had gone from bartender to short order cook, and much preferred the younger clientele. She was a single mother of forty with a six year old boy in elementary school. Sherri had come to Ernie and Brenda two years ago and told them she was trying to put her life back together. She needed a job that wasn't in a bar, so she could raise her son the right way. They hired her immediately, and invited her and her son Bobby to church the following Sunday morning.

"Leave the boy alone, Sis. This is my new Superintendent, R.J. He started this morning. R.J. say hello to Sherri, the Manager of the trendiest diner on Sharon Ave."

R.J. nodded quietly.

"What'll it be boys?" she asked.

After lunch, Ernie and R.J. spent the afternoon doing some banking business.

"I got one more set of sagging steps over in Hancock. Got any energy left?" Ernie asked.

"Bring it on," said R.J.

Twenty minutes later they pulled up in front of Kitty's house and Ernie said, "I think it's this one on the right. It looks like it could use a little fixing up."

"Yer da Boss," R.J. said as they got out of the truck.

R.J. carried a half a dozen new two by sixes up to the porch, and started tearing off the old steps with a crow bar. Suddenly the front door opened.

"What the … R.J. Hi, how are you, come on in, please." Kitty shouted, rushing out in her stocking feet and throwing her arms around his neck.

"Come on Ma, yer gonna freeze to death. I'll come inside in a minute, okay, I got work to do. This is my boss Ernie," he said to her. "Ernie, this is my mom. Now go inside." He said to her, "Yer gonna catch cold."

Kitty rubbed her shoulders and ran in the front door. She put some coffee on and sat by the front window to watch her son fix her front porch. He looked so handsome in his coveralls.

Thirty minutes later, with a new set of steps a new railing, and several boards replaced on the porch, Ernie and R.J. put their tools and board scraps into the bed of the truck.

"Do you suppose we've got time to drop in and say hello," Ernie said.

R.J. smiled as he brushed saw dust off of his Carharts and walked up the new steps. Kitty threw her arms around Ernie as he came through the front door.

"I'm sorry R.J. but when Johnny told me all of the wonderful things that this man and his wife have done to help us, well I'm just so grateful to them both I don't know what to say."

"Don't say anything Kitty," Ernie said, "but if that's hot coffee I smell I think that might warm us up a bit."

The three chatted for a while and Ernie thanked Kitty for the coffee. He told her that the lumber had been anonymously donated, and that the work was a labor of love donated by her son. Kitty cried. She hugged both men, and they rode back to Houghton without saying a word.

"I don't know how to thank you," said R.J. as he got out of the truck at the jail.

"See you in the morning, brother," said Ernie.

Johnny personally called everyone involved on Wednesday morning and gave them a detailed report of his trip to Gaylord. Everyone agreed the ball was now in R.J.'s court and what ever he wanted to do with his future was in his hands. Johnny's last call was to Maggie.

"Maggie this is Johnny, how's the patient?"

"Well, he's doing lots of sleeping and that's a good thing," she said. "I suppose you want to talk to him."

"No, I think your first advice of letting him rest and keeping him calm made the most sense. So, I'll tell you what I know, and you can decide what's best for Howard. How's that."

"Thank you, Johnny. I really appreciate your concern. You know until the other day, I never realized he's all I've really got."

"And that's why we love you both Maggie and want you both to heal and have a full life. So, let me know if there's anything any of us can do for either of you, okay."

"Okay and thank you Johnny"

"Maggie, will you pray with me?"

"Now," she asked.

> *"Father God Maggie and Howard are so important to everyone who know and love them. Wrap your loving arms around them and protect them and bless them Father, Amen."*

"Take care Maggie." Johnnie hung up.

The cigarette smoke in the cab of Robert's old Dodge truck was so thick that the two drunks in the back couldn't even see the dash lights, but neither noticed. All of the men had passed out an hour ago and the sound of four open mouths snoring like Husqvarna chain saws cutting through green pine only added a symphonic ambiance to this degenerative quartet. They were awaiting the opening of firearm deer season on a lumber trail off of Highway 26 just east of Eagle River. The salt licks and apples had been dragged out to their hunting site last week, and Eino and Little Harold had been down there twice this week at sunset with binoculars looking for big racks. Robert said if they moved in before day light they could hit them with spot lights and be out of there by dawn. They all knew this was illegal, but that didn't matter to these guys. If they were lucky, they could shoot as many as they could then hang them and gut them in the swamp. Bernie had the only legal permit between them, so he would take the biggest one home. It was cold enough for the rest of the kill to hang on poles for days without anyone being the wiser. Eino coughed a couple of times from the back seat and it was obvious that he wasn't going to die from old age.

Bernie's wristwatch alarm went off at 5:00 a.m. and the slow process of four semi- comatose drunks trying to rally their bodies to action began. Like synchronized swimmers the four doors opened at one time as the would-be shooters took care of nature's call, not to mention letting most of the foul air out of the cab. A meeting was held at the front bumper as four new cigarettes were lit along with the intermittent coughing that ensued. The game plan was to stealthily sneak down into the swamp with their weapons and battery operated spot lights and wait for the herd to make its early morning run to the feed. Robert led the way as usual and the men settled in behind some rotted out logs. A rather sticky half pint of butterscotch schnapps was passed from gloved hand to gloved hand. A twig snapped deeper in the swamp and the men froze in position.

Years of training taught by grandfathers and fathers suddenly kicked in as the soldiers readied themselves. No one moved as at first the does came into the small clearing and looked around. They were barely visible, but eyes that were trained by experience watched as the deer slowly moved towards the bait. No one moved. Real hunters will tell you that this is the best part of the hunt. You can feel your nerves start to tense up hoping the biggest buck you have ever seen will stick his head around a tree and come walking out right at you. And you keep waiting. Nobody moves a muscle. And then, as if it was all a game, the herd casually moves out and starts eating. The four assassins picked out their primary targets, hit the flood lights and the bloodbath began. Two big bucks went down and another was hit and ran. Three does were hit on the second volley, but the shots were hurried and two were dragging their hind quarters. And then it was over. Little Harold took off after the errant buck following a blood trail, knowing that the deer would bleed out before too long. The other three walked towards the killing field with a look of satisfaction. Once again, there would be a couple of big racks on the back wall of the barn and plenty of venison for the holidays. They would shoot a few more after Christmas to get them through the winter and life would go on.

Two hours later, five deer were gutted and hanging on deer poles in the swamp as the snow began to fall. Robert, Bernie, Eino, and Little Harold took a break and then dragged the largest buck up out of the swamp along with the two other racks to their truck where a Conservation Officer and a State Police cruiser had them blocked in. Robert Hackala knew they had been had.

The State trooper refused to put the four violators in his cruiser because they were covered with deer blood, so he put them in Robert's truck after taking all of their driver licenses. He told them to report to the Houghton County Jail by noon with clean clothes on.

Bill Cooder, the C.O., called for back up and went down into the swamp to find the remaining kill. These deer would be cut up and given to the needy, as well as all of the other illegal game taken during the season.

There was no celebration down at Shute's Bar in Calumet that evening among the local hunters because four of the local denizens were in the hoosegow. There was plenty of talk about an inside informant who might have turned the poachers in, but no one could agree on any one in particular. The two leading candidates were Bernie and Eino's wives who had often complained about living with men who never worked or took baths and spent most of their time sitting in bars lying about one thing or another, but no one could prove anything. So, the gang at Shute's just sat around and felt bad about losing those three big racks, without even knowing how big they really were.

Sometimes the stories that were told on cold night around Shute's Bar had unhappy endings.

"You got company R.J." said Ron as R.J. returned from work on Saturday.

"Anybody I know?" R.J. asked.

"You might be surprised," Ron answered as he led R.J. back to the lock-up cells.

The cells facing his had two prisoners in each, with three men sitting on the edges of their bunks, and one lying on the top facing the wall. Officer Burch let R.J. in and locked the cell door.

"Are you just coming in?" asked Eino from across the room.

"No," said R.J. I have a work permit during the day time and just spend my nights here."

"How'd you get a deal like that?" asked Bernie.

"It took a long time," R.J. answered, but I hope it's only temporary."

"Say," Eino said, "aren't you R.J. Hackala?"

"That's right," said R.J.

"Hey Robert, say hello to yer boy," said Eino, and Robert rolled over on the top bunk and smiled at his son.

"How ya doin R.J.?" asked Robert as he slid down and stood by the bars.

"Fine dad," R.J. answered. "What are you doin in here?"

"Oh, we had a little misunderstanding about some deer this morning and it'll probably take a judge to straighten it out." Robert said with a smirk on his face. "Say hello to yer grandpa, R.J."

"Is that you Grandpa Harold? I ain't seen you in a long time. How ya been?" R.J. asked.

Little Harold sat on the end of the bunk as if it wasn't at all unusual to be in jail with Robert. "I been fine R.J., been reading all about you and Jimmy."

Bernie and Eino both grinned like it was a big joke and the laugh was going to be on the judge come Monday morning.

"Have you been up to see Jimmy?" R.J. asked Robert.

"I've been thinkin on it, but I haven't been in town lately, and I'm sure your mother would have something to say on the subject."

"Probably so," R.J. said covering up for Robert's lack of interest.

"You boys deserved a lot better shake than you got, but you know there wasn't nothing I could do about it 'cause the law was on yer mother's side. They got those laws fixed so that the women got all the rights. There just ain't nothing that a man can do about it, son. You know what I mean."

"I understand, Dad," R.J. said to keep from embarrassing his father in front of his dad.

R.J. stared at the four men and sadly realized that he would probably have ended up like them if it hadn't of been for Johnny.

"Well fellas, I had a long day. I think I'll catch some sleep and we'll talk some more tomorrow. Good night guys, Good night Dad, good night grandpa."

R.J. pulled the blanket over his head to block out the light, and began talking to his new friend.

> *"God, I don't get it. If I had been raised by my dad instead of my mom, I would probably be sleeping in the same jail, but in a different cell. Was it me or was it them? Are these jails full of kids who never had a fair shot or is it our own fault. You sure got a lot to teach me, but I'm ready to learn. God, don't be too hard on my mom or my dad. I don't think either one of them had much of a chance either. Good night Lord."*

R.J. woke up early the next morning and saw his dad staring at him through the bars.

"Do you remember when you and me and Jimmy used to slide down the hill in the winter time in Laurium, Dad?"

"I sure do, son. Those were happier times."

$$\underline{\text{\scriptsize ☀}}$$

CHAPTER 20

"What are we going to do for Thanksgiving?" asked Helen as Johnny escorted her and Jenny down the steps after church on Sunday morning.

"It's kind of a tradition in our family to have Turkey pasties in honor of the Finns who came over on the Mayflowerinen," said Johnny.

"I'm not sure why we even bother to take this boy to Mass," said Jenny. He's so evil."

"I agree," Said Helen, "but he always takes us out to lunch."

"Small sacrifice for such interesting company," Jenny retorted as they got in the van.

"Do you think your folks would come up?" Helen asked Johnny as they drove towards Houghton.

"I doubt it," Johnny replied, "They'd have to be back by Sunday."

"Jenny, I'm sure you're probably going home to Laurium for dinner aren't you?"

"Not this year," Jenny replied, "my folks are going to my dad's side of the family in Green Bay."

"I have a suggestion." Johnny said.

Both of the ladies looked at him.

"How would the two of you ladies like to have dinner at the Hendricks' next Thursday?"

"You're kidding," said Helen.

"In Grand Rapids?" Jenny said.

"Furniture Capital of the World," chimed in Johnny the smart aleck. "My mom invited you both, and we have lots of room to put you up. Plus I would consider it a personal favor. You two have shown me your town, now I would like to show you mine. We can leave early Wednesday morning and come back on Monday. Please say yes or you'll both break a poor troll's heart."

"We'll have to split the cost of gas," Helen said.

"I would insist," Johnny said facetiously.

"What will we wear?" Jenny chimed in.

"I would leave that up to your discretion. Nothing too trashy I hope."

"Oh Johnny, I've always wanted to see southern Michigan." Jenny oozed.

"Well, stick with me kids," Johnny said in his best Bogart interpretation. "Then it's a deal?" he asked as he pulled into the Perkins parking lot in Houghton.

"Yes", they both said at the same time.

"Good," he said, "Now let's eat. I'm starved."

Johnny called Angie from the restaurant and handed the phone to Helen.

"Is this my dear friend Helen?" Angie asked.

"Yes it is," said Helen.

"We're so excited that you and Jenny are coming for Thanksgiving. Don't worry about anything. I'll have both of your rooms made up and on Friday we'll go shopping all day in downtown Grand Rapids. It will be great. I can hardly wait.

"If you're sure we won't be too much trouble?" Helen said.

"Trouble?" Angie asked, "We'll have a ball, I promise. Now let me say hi to Jenny." Helen passed the phone to Jenny and smiled at Johnny who was devouring his salad.

Johnny woke out of a sound sleep and caught the phone on the third ring.

"I suppose you're going to lie in bed all day" the unknown voice said.

"Who is this," asked Johnny sitting up trying to clear his head.

"It's Howard. Don't tell me my voice is that weak," he laughed.

It really was, but Johnny didn't want him to know it. "Of course not Howard, I think it's just a bad connection. How are you feeling? I'm pleasantly surprised to hear your voice."

"Maggie told me you had called and gave me the run down on your trip to Gaylord, but I thought I would rather hear it from the horse's mouth." He laughed.

"Ask Maggie if you're up to a short visit," Johnny said.

"She said any time," Howard responded. "She claims I'm driving her crazy."

"Well, how about if I drop in around 10:00 a.m. and we'll have a little chat."

"That would be perfect Johnny. By the way, she told me you prayed for us. That really meant a lot. I mean it, Johnny." Howard said with more emotion than Johnny expected.

"I'll see you later this morning, Howard" said Johnny, sensing a change in Howard's demeanor.

Johnny pulled in the driveway and remembered the last time he was there. It seemed a life time ago, and maybe it was in terms of where Maggie and Howard now were. Maggie met him at the door and embraced him.

"Johnny Hendricks, you are changing a lot of lives in this town. Bless you for that."

"Praise God from whom all blessing flow, Maggie. How's the patient?"

"To tell you the truth, he seems like a changed man. I don't know whether that trip to the hospital scared him, or God touched him, but he's not the same old Howard. I can tell you that."

"Maybe he just got tired of running into a wall all the time. It happens you know."

"I can hear you two talking about me," Howard shouted from the couch in the living room.

Johnny and Maggie walked through the kitchen into the presence of a rejuvenated but weakened man lying on the couch. Howard's eyes sparkled as Johnny pulled up a chair next to him.

"How are you my friend?" Johnny said, taking Howard's hand.

"I've got so much to tell you," said Howard.

"I can see it in your eyes. Your life has changed. How do you feel?"

"Johnny, you were the last person I saw that night before I almost died." Howard's eyes started to water and his hands began shaking. "I remember that night so vividly. I thought the world was against me. I was so full of hate for my wife and her family and self-pity for me. And you, you listened to me and offered to pray for me to ease my pain."

Tears were streaming down Howard's face and his body was trembling. "I could have died that night. Alone." Howard reached up and took Maggie's hand. "I'm so ashamed. I drove this wonderful woman out of her own house. You know, I think I wanted to die that night. When I finally hit the bottom I couldn't stand myself." He squeezed Maggie's hand, and wiped away the tears with the sleeve of his pajamas. "And then, the next day, when I saw her face in the Emergency Room, I finally realized how much I really loved her, more than anything else in the world. Johnny at that moment I knew I had to live to make things right for all the mistakes I had made over the years." Howard paused, and my young friend I need you to help me do that. Do you understand what I'm trying to tell you, Johnny?"

Johnny took Maggie's other hand in his and with tears running down all their faces he bowed his head and prayed,

> *"Father God we open our hearts to you that You might fill us with the peace that passeth understanding. Help us to accept Your grace and lead us to do Your perfect will Amen."*

The three quietly held hands and shared a moment that they would never forget. Maggie broke the spell by offering to run up to Tony's in Laurium for pasties. Howard and Johnny thought that was a great idea.

Maggie left with the lunch order and Johnny brought Howard a fresh glass of ice water from the kitchen.

"You know, Johnny, this prayer thing is brand new to me. We never had it at home as a kid cause we didn't need it. We had everything else. We had money, power, and social position our whole lives up in Laurium. Only the poor miners went to church. Religion was for the poor lower-class folks. That's just the way it was."

"And now?" Johnny asked.

"I don't know, but it sure seems to be working for everybody else. I know I'd sure like some of what you got," Howard said jokingly. "We've got lots of time to talk about what I've got later, but for now, let me catch you up on what's going on in your world, okay?"

The two men discussed the Gaylord meeting and how it affected all concerned. They talked about Jimmy and R.J. and also how Kitty fit into the picture. Johnny mentioned that the city inspection team had started working on the Aho Building and it looked like rewiring and new plumbing were a possibility to bring the old place up to code, but it would be into December before anybody could come up with some solid figures.

"So, it looks like we're heading in the right direction on every front. Our biggest challenge is to get you and Jimmy up and moving. R.J. should be squared away with his responsibilities by Christmas and settled into the Suggs home. I'm not sure if I'm happy with Kitty and Jimmy living alone at her place this winter, but we'll have to see how that works out."

Just then Maggie came in the side door with two big bags from Tony's and set them on the kitchen table.

"Give me a hand, Johnny," she said. "I got a hungry man to feed in there."

"Is she always this bossy?" Johnny asked Howard.

"I don't know how I put up with her," he said, and they all laughed.

"You put up with me because I was the only girl in Hancock who gave that poor mining boy from Laurium a second look," Maggie said as she carried in the tray of pasties from the kitchen.

"I guess she told you," said Johnny following her with a tray of coffee and cups.

While they ate lunch Johnny suggested that maybe he and Maggie could pick up Kitty and go visit Jimmy while Howard took his afternoon nap.

"Sounds like a great idea" said Howard. "Tell Jimmy I'm really looking forward to seeing him, and this time I mean it."

Maggie looked up over the rim of her coffee cup and winked at Johnny.

An hour later the three caught Jimmy riding up the elevator in his wheel chair from physical therapy and Aunt Maggie bent down and kissed him on the cheek.

"Don't think I didn't see the way you were looking at that nurse getting off the elevator," said Aunt Maggie in a mock scolding tone.

"Oh that was just Nancy, she's my P.T. nurse."

"I know who she is. Uncle Howard looked at her that way too when he was in physical therapy. You men aren't fooling anybody. That's all I'm saying," Maggie joked.

Jimmy shook his head in mock desperation as the elevator door opened and he pushed himself down the hallway to his room. Without any assistance he climbed into his bed and pulled up the sheet.

"When do they say I can go home, Mom?" Jimmy asked, seemingly for the hundredth time.

"The speech therapist says you're fine, but the physical therapist wants to see you get a little stronger on those stairs, and so do I."

"R.J. told me he built some brand new steps just for me," Jimmy said excitedly.

"When did you see him?" asked Kitty.

"Oh he and Ernie drop in when they are working in the area. He brought me a milk shake yesterday afternoon. He told me he bought it with his own money. He works you know."

"Yes honey, he's a carpenter. That's a pretty important job," Kitty smiled. "Maybe someday you can be his helper, huh."

"He said I gotta finish school first." Jimmy said.

"Well, I'm sure he's right," said Kitty proudly.

CHAPTER 21

"What in the world is in this over night bag Helen, your rock collection?" Johnny asked as he tried to lift it into the back of the van.

"Johnny, I don't know where you were brought up, but in civilized society you don't visit people without bringing a little something as a gift," Helen said sharply.

"What did you bring, Brockway Mountain?"

"Just put it in the back and stop making such a fuss. You'll wake up the whole neighborhood," Helen said going for another load.

Jenny took his arm, gave him a kiss, and said, "Relax, it's only half of Brockway Mountain, big guy."

"It's your loss," Johnny said. "Brockway was the nicest thing in Copper Harbor."

Fully loaded and on the road at 7:30 a.m., Johnny gassed up in Houghton and everyone was in a great mood as they headed south.

"You know I never thought I'd ever see the Lower Peninsula," Helen said from the back seat. "I don't know how to thank you Johnny. This is like a dream for me."

"If you hadn't of opened your door last month and let that troll in out of the cold, I probably wouldn't be here either Helen," Johnnie said. "Thank you for being such a good neighbor and a good friend."

The ladies dozed most of the way across the Upper Peninsula, and by 2:00 pm they were in Gaylord where Johnny showed them the court house where R.J. got his freedom. They had lunch and jumped from I-75 to US 131 and at 7:00 p.m. three travel-weary Yoopers pulled into the driveway of John and Angie Hendricks' home.

"Are there any survivors?" John asked, opening Jenny's door.

Angie helped Helen out of the back seat, and it was all any one could do to stand up.

"I'll be fine," moaned Johnny. "Just see to the women and children." Nobody laughed.

"Come in, come in," Angie said. "John and Grandpa will get the luggage."

Johnny carried the bags up to the bed room and the ladies followed.

"I thought you might be more comfortable in this big room with twin beds and a bathroom, than one up and one down. I hope its okay."

"It's perfect," Jenny said. "You're very considerate."

"Nothing's too good for our son's two sidekicks," Angie joked. "Go ahead and freshen up. John's built a big fire in the fireplace in the den, and I've got a pot of chili and a pan of corn bread in the oven if you're hungry. Take your time, we'll be down stairs," Angie said as she closed the door.

"Wow," Jenny said, "what great people. This might be the best vacation I've ever had" she said as she began unpacking her suitcase.

"Come right in," Grandpa said invitingly" as Helen and Jenny entered the den. "Can I offer you both a glass of fresh apple cider, pressed right here in Kent County?"

"That would be wonderful," said Helen, she paused. "With three Johns in the room, do you have a nickname I could call you maybe?" she asked Grandpa.

"Well, when my wife was alive she and my close friends used to call me "Dutch". I would be pleased to hear that name again, Helen," Grandpa smiled.

"Dutch, you know, that suits you," Helen said. "The name has a certain character about it."

"He's a character alright," said Angie, entering the room with a tray of cheese and crackers. "Dinner will be ready in a few minutes, but first I'd like to hear about your little twelve hour junket from the northland."

Everyone ate their fill while Helen and Jenny told stories about Johnny's treacherous driving. Dinner ensued and it wasn't long before the yawns took over the conversation, and everybody went to bed.

Helen and Jenny both woke up at 9:30 a.m. and were shocked and embarrassed that they had slept so long. They both threw on their clothes and rushed down the stairs.

"Good morning," Angie welcomed. The family was relaxing and sitting around a table of Dutch apple strudel and hot coffee. "I hope you both slept well," Dutch said.

"The best night sleep I've had in a long time," said Jenny.

"Happy Turkey Day," said Johnny," I just set the timer on the bird, and now we have until later this afternoon to relax, and maybe take a little ride around G.R. and see the sights."

"That's a great idea," said Dad. "Sit down ladies and take a little nourishment then we'll clean up and hit the road. I'm sure you're both anxious to get back into a car," he said with a smile.

Two hours later the five of them were driving down Fulton Street hill into downtown Grand Rapids. Grandpa and Angie elected to stay home to watch the turkey and set the table. Helen was amazed at how modern the city center was. When she saw the huge Alexander Calder sculpture she asked John to park the car so she could take a picture. They drove past the new hockey arena and down along the Grand River. The sun came out through the clouds and a brief shower of crystalline snow blew across the windshield. It was obvious that God was happy to have Jenny and Helen down for Thanksgiving. John drove over to the old neighborhood where he and Angie started their first church, and several people waved as they drove by.

"Take them by our old house, Dad," Johnny said as they pulled around the corner on Oak Street. The old two story houses reminded Jenny of where she grew up in Laurium. Johnny pointed out the house he grew up in. Dad slowed down to see if anyone was living there.

"That's my bedroom on this end of the second floor," Johnny pointed out. "I had model airplanes hanging from the ceiling and all of my scout projects on display. I was a pretty amazing kid, wasn't I, Dad? Dad?"

"I'm sorry Johnny. I didn't quite hear what you said." John said, winking at Helen. "I think we'd better head for home and give Mom a hand setting the table," John said. "I'll bet the whole house smells like turkey."

An hour later Grandpa said grace and Dad carved the bird. Everyone at the table took turns telling the others about a memorable Thanksgiving from their past. Helen was quite emotional telling about her first Thanksgiving with Arvin and little Stevie, and Angie put her hand on Helen's to comfort her through her memory. Jenny's stories were full of noisy relatives, venison neck roasts and too much to drink which lifted everybody's spirits. Grandpa talked more about the early days of their ministries and helping others, and that sort of balanced out the conversation. After the main course, Angie told everyone to head for the den for pumpkin pie and coffee, and they were all grateful for the chance to stand and rearrange their dinner.

Later in the evening, Angie told Helen and Jenny that the Friday after Thanksgiving was also a holiday. "In the civilized world," she said, "tomorrow is the official start of Christmas shopping for all women who are able. Do you feel able?" She asked Helen.

"You betcha," Helen answered.

"You can count me in, too," said Jenny.

"Then it's a deal. We'll leave the boys to their own devices, eh." said Angie.

Johnny woke up at 8:00 a.m. and the house was quiet. He came downstairs and joined his Dad at the kitchen table.

"I guess we missed the rush earlier this morning," Johnny said pouring himself an orange juice.

"They were out the door with their credit cards stuck in their teeth before I could even say good morning. I think it must be something in their genetics, son."

"I assume you preach on that character flaw on occasion," Johnny remarked.

Dad looked up over his coffee cup. "Yeah sure."

"What's the game plan for the day?" asked Grandpa coming into the dining room.

"I thought we might go over to the church and have Johnny give some of the board members an update this morning on the state of the union, or should I say state of the Yooper union. I knew the girls were going shopping this morning, Johnny, so I called a few people so you could tell them how things are going. I hope you don't mind."

"No, that's perfect, Dad. I'm kind of proud of our progress."

Two hours later the three men walked into the church fellowship hall and were greeted by a half dozen old friends who Johnny hadn't seen in a few months.

"Welcome everyone," Pastor John said good naturedly. "I hope you all took sufficient nourishment yesterday so that we won't have to send out for doughnuts this morning."

Everyone smiled at the corny remark dished out by their Pastor.

"As you can see, our representative from the north woods has returned for a little of his Mom's cooking, and about two month's worth of laundry," he paused. This drew a bigger laugh and a grin from Johnny. "Anyway, here's Johnny to give us a run down and answer any questions we might have about our future mission up in Hancock. Johnny?"

The other eight people at the table gave Johnny a big round of applause, which made him feel like the work that he had done so far was appreciated and that God was leading him in the right direction.

"It sure is great to see you all this morning and to make one correction; I only brought one month's worth of laundry with me. I left the other one for Christmas." This brought a bigger laugh than his father received, and Grandpa slapped Dad on the back.

"Angie and I can hardly wait," Dad said, to the guffaws of everyone.

When the laughter subsided, Johnny said, "In all seriousness, if it weren't for the people at this table, and the many good folks who you represent, the positive groundwork done in Hancock led by the Hand of God could not have been accomplished. I will always be grateful for your prayers and donations through this difficult month and a half."

Johnny began his story and left out very little. He told them about meeting Helen and lodging with her. He told them about Jenny with her influences at MTU and the radio station as well as showing him the peninsula and its history. He mentioned Bob Heikinen, Howard Berg, all of the clergy in the HHCA, and also his connections with law enforcement in the area. He was very emotional when he told them about the Hackala family and how God had brought them through a very difficult situation and then allowed Johnny to help bring them home to Jesus Christ.

"Finally my dear friends, we come to the mission. Bob Heikinen told me before I left Hancock that the Aho Building is basically sound. We already have the finances and the workers to do the wiring and the plumbing, so that with God's grace, we will be able to get in there after the first of the year and start making it usable."

"How 'bout we get a refill on the coffees and then maybe Johnny can answer some questions," John said, pulling his chair away from the table.

Ten minutes later, Mildred DeWitt from the Finance Committee asked, "Johnny, I think you're doing an amazing job, but how long do you think our church will need to keep financing this project, Honey? I mean, I'm not asking for myself, but I'm sure there are people who will want to know. After all, it's a long ways away. Do you know what I mean?"

Grandpa stared at Mildred. "What are you trying to say Mildred? Do you think we should charge them interest?"

"No, Dutch, but it's not like they're from Africa or somewhere. I mean they're just Americans, you know?"

"Mildred, here's our plan," Johnny cut in. "Once we become successful, and hopefully that will be soon, we will solicit the city. We will have fund raisers and create ways to generate money in every quarter to make ourselves self-sufficient. When that day comes, representatives from our church will be invited up to Hancock and honored for their Christian spirit and generosity."

"Oh, well that would be nice," Mildred said.

Terry Gimbel, looking down his nose at Mildred, asked, "Is there anything we can do now to help, Johnny?"

"No, Terry, just you're prayers and good wishes. You've all been wonderful. Thank you. If there are no more questions, would you all pray with me?"

> *"Dear God. With positive people like these, we*
> *can change the world. We in the mission field are*
> *so grateful that You allow us all to work together*
> *for Your greater good. Amen."*

Johnny thanked them all for coming and walked Mildred out to her car.

The three shoppers dragged through the door about 2:00 p.m., exhausted.

"It was brutal out there," exclaimed Angie.

"I never saw so many stores in my life," said Helen.

"And the bargains," said Jenny. "I've never saved so much money."

"It's amazing the things that women have to do just to maintain traditions at the holidays," said Johnny, helping the ladies carry in the shopping bags. "We men don't appreciate how fortunate we are to be spared all of that torture."

"I've always thought that it was better to be the hunter than the gatherer," joined in Grandpa, with tongue in cheek.

"Well I hope you girls won't be too tired for dinner at Jose Babusksa's this evening," Dad said. "I was just going to make reservations."

"I don't think I want to put my shoes back on," said Angie.

"Why don't we let Johnny and Jenny go out on the town and let us old folks stay in for the night," suggested Helen.

"That sounds like a better plan," said Johnny.

"If the rest of you don't mind?" added Jenny.

"Consider it a done deal," said Dad, and they all relaxed.

"What sounds good?" Johnny said backing out of the driveway.

"Anything but pasties," Jenny said, leaning over and kissing him on the cheek.

As they drove through Johnny's old suburban neighborhood they both enjoyed the extravagant Christmas light displays with each house trying to outdo the next.

"How long did you live here?" Jenny asked him as she took his right hand in hers.

"All through high school and college," he said feeling the warmth from her hands.

"Tell me about growing up here?" she asked.

"Don't you want to go eat?" he said quietly.

"Not yet," She said. "I just want to know more about you. Why don't you pull over by the curb and we can talk."

"Okay. Ask me anything you want." He said with a false bravado.

"You know Johnny, you're the sweetest guy I've ever met, but I don't know anything about you. You're always strong. You always know what to say and what to do. You always laugh and joke, but you never let me in. I wish I could get as close to you as you are to God."

"No, I don't think you would want to do that" he said quietly. "I'm not the person you think I am. Believe me life is a lot better if you just allow me to be good old Johnny. The past is better off staying where it is."

"Please Johnny," she said softly as the snow covered the windshield.

"It was my fault," he said letting go of her hand, "even though the State Police said it wasn't. I should have been driving slower, or I could have been driving slower. It came out of nowhere. I hit it head on, but I lost control and hit a tree, that's all I know."

"What are you talking about Johnny?" Jenny asked, suddenly concerned.

"We were having such fun. Bill and Mary, me and Amy were always together, ever since tenth grade. Bill and I were best buddies and Amy and Mary were our first real girl friends. Do you know what love is like in the eleventh grade?" Johnny asked. "It consumes you. You can't breathe, or think about anything else. It was the happiest time of our lives."

Silence filled the inside of Johnny's van as his memory refused to let him tell the rest of the story. Jenny rubbed his neck and felt the sobbing begin. The flood walls that held back the agony of nearly eight years broke as he wailed Amy's name over and over. Johnny grabbed Jenny and hugged her harder than he had ever held anyone before, and she hugged him back like a mother hugs a devastated child.

"Amy went through the windshield, and Bill in the back seat went right over the top of her." Johnny stared at the blank white window through his tears. They both died immediately.

I got a concussion and was in a coma for two weeks. When I came out of it, my girl and my best friend were both buried two miles from here. Mary wasn't hurt and I had a scar on my head that was all."

This wild flashback from the past had stunned Jenny into silence. It was getting cold so Johnny started the van and turned on the windshield wipers. There was nothing more for him to say. The heat was blowing over him and Jenny, and the wiper blades were plowing nice even rows on either side of the windshield. From out of nowhere the self loathing began. The monster had been released. He had nowhere to hide now. Johnny the monster, that nice young youth pastor with such a bright future had finally been revealed for who he really was. He was simply a murderer, and anything else anyone wanted to say or believe about him was a lie. He shivered for a second, and vomited all over himself, and sat in silence with spittle dripping from his chin.

Jenny called Helen from the van and told her to have John and Grandpa come and pick them up. Two hours later at Spectrum Hospital in downtown Grand Rapids all five sat in the visitor's room as the doctors evaluated Johnny.

Shortly after midnight, Dr. Evans came out to talk to the family.

"I trust you are all family," he said.

"You can tell us all what ever it is Doctor," said John.

"I've got to confess I've only seen this condition two times, once after Viet Nam, and the other time was a PTSD victim from Falusia, Iraq. Johnny has been carrying this horror and guilt for a very long time and it was never diagnosed or treated. How he has buried this inside for so long is difficult to understand. He seems to have been able to forget it and pay it forward, if you will, through good works. I know it's hard to understand and maybe this is a bit simplistic, but that's as much as I can make of it at this time. Suffice it to say, we would like to keep him for a while and try to ease some of these demons."

"Of course doctor, of course," said John. "Can we see him?"

"We're trying to keep him calm without too much sedation, but he said something about saying good night to Jenny. Are you Jenny?" Evans asked.

Jenny entered Johnny's room. The lights were dim and Johnny was lying in bed.

"I guess I owe you a dinner," Johnny said sheepishly.

"And it better not be a pastie," Jenny said with a grin.

"Well, never a dull moment with old crazy Johnny, huh," he said.

"Johnny, the doctor told me I can't stay too long, but you are more special to me now than you ever were. All I want now is a kiss and a prayer, and I will be up to see you tomorrow morning, okay?"

"You probably say that to all the guys," he quipped, but the sadness hadn't left his eyes.

> *"Dear God, we put ourselves in your hands and*
> *ask only for the opportunity to serve. We thank*
> *you Lord for a wonderful day. Amen."*

"Say good night to everybody," he said, "and I'll see you all in the morning. Good night." Johnny rolled over towards the wall, and with tears leaking from his eyes, he pulled the pillow over his head.

CHAPTER 22

"I don't know what to say, Jenny. It was a long time ago." Angie said as they pulled away from the huge Spectrum Hospital complex and headed east towards their home.

"We thought that he had worked his way through it, but apparently the coming home and the time of year brought it all back," John said.

They all sat silently and waited for a red light to change. The snow had let up, but the rear tires slid a little before gaining traction as John pulled away from the intersection.

"I feel so responsible," said Jenny. "I was asking Johnny about growing up in Grand Rapids, and he started talking about high school"… she paused.

"God works in mysterious ways Jenny," Grandpa said. "When Johnny regained consciousness after the accident, his whole world changed. His girlfriend and his best buddy were gone, and although he never said it, he felt responsible. He and Mary were never able to deal with it, and she transferred to another school the next term. And,"

Grandpa sighed, "the whole school embraced and supported Johnny and put him in a position where he couldn't grieve or sort out his feelings in that whole terrible mess. We were partially responsible for not getting him the psychological help he needed to get rid of some of those demons, but he was doing so well," Grandpa paused, letting the thought hang in the air.

"Jenny, before the accident Johnny was just an average kid with average grades, no ambition and no direction." Dad said.

"And afterwards?" Jenny asked, as if this might help piece together a broken puzzle.

"Well afterwards, he was like he is now. He changed. He began living for everyone else," John continued. "It was as if the world was his responsibility."

"And his relationship with God changed," said Angie. "I mean, he prayed all the time. I imagine he still does, Am I right?"

"Absolutely," said Helen from the dark corner of the back seat. "He's the most spiritual person I've ever met," she said. "I love him like my own son."

"I didn't know you had a son," said Angie.

"Ya, he's buried right next to Arvin," she said as a quietness fell over the car. "He came back from Viet Nam, but no one could help him either. I called the V.A. Medical Center in Iron Mountain, but they said he wasn't wounded and there were lots of vets coming home that were a little messed up. Father at church tried to talk to him, but Stevie just laughed at him and told him he had no idea what was going on over there. Doctors at the V.A. sent him drugs to relax him, but he only got more agitated. The coroner said it was accidental drowning and I agreed. No autopsy was ever going to bring my son back."

Jenny put her arm around Helen and tried to comfort her as the older woman wept.

"What a sad night," said John as they pulled into the driveway.

Angie came down the stairs at 3:00 a.m. and saw a light on in the den.

"If I'm disturbing you Helen, I'll leave, but I thought we might have a nice cup of green tea to soothe our souls," Angie said.

"Don't make a fuss, but if you're going to have one I'll share the tea bag." Helen said.

A few minutes later Angie came back with two steaming mugs of tea and a plate of Windmill cookies. "These are my favorites with tea," she said, offering the plate to Helen.

"I apologize for adding to your discomfort this evening, Angie. I'm afraid my timing wasn't very good."

"You know it's funny you should say that Helen. Actually your timing was perfect. You see, I also lost someone very dear to me about that time, and I'm embarrassed to say that I don't think about him often enough anymore."

Helen set down her mug and looked at Angie. The story of Angie's youth and her escape to the United States began to unfold. The part of her story she seldom told was about her younger brother Jose who along with a friend had traveled to Ciudad Juarez to try and enter the United States through El Paso. Her parents had never heard if he made it through the border or if he disappeared in Mexico before he got there. He and his friend were just two of the thousands of people who vanished while trying to start a new life.

"It embarrasses me that I don't speak more about him or keep his memory alive. I only pray that if he is still alive he is at peace," Angie said.

"You know Angie, I'm not a spiritual person, but I think maybe God dragged up all of our pasts tonight to give us all a fresh start as we approach the Advent Season."

"I hope you're right Helen. I know I sure couldn't stand another night like tonight," Angie said. "Anyway I'm sure glad that God put you in our Johnny's life to help and guide him on his first real trip away from home. You are a real blessing to all of us."

"Thank you Angie. That tea made me sleepy. I hope tomorrow isn't a shopping day."

Angie turned out the lights in the den as the two friends went upstairs back to bed.

The phone rang at 9:00 a.m. and John caught it on the second ring.

"Good morning," said John.

"It's me, Dad. The sawbones' just finished their walk through and gave me my walking papers. I chatted with the head shrink who had consulted with Doctor Evans from last night, and both agreed that my hanging around the hospital for the weekend would do no one any good. So, I'm good to go. If you can pick me up in a half hour, I'll be standing by the front door.

"I'll see you in a little while son," said Dad as he hung up the phone.

"Who was that?" said Angie rolling over in bed.

"That was Johnny. They cleared him to come home. I'm going to pick him up right now," he said.

"Do you want me to come with you?" asked Angie.

"No, I think he and I need to have a little father and son time, but I think we'll be ready for breakfast when we get back."

John pulled up to the hospital entrance, and Johnny jumped in.

"Here, you'd better put this on," Dad said handing Johnny a hooded sweatshirt. "Your coat from last night is a little worse for wear."

"Yeah, that part of the evening's a little foggy, and also a little embarrassing. I'm not quite sure what happened, but all of a sudden that big old deer was right in front of me again, and I hit the brakes, but I couldn't miss him. I don't know why Dad. I haven't thought about that in years. It was terrible. I could still hear Amy screaming as we slid down that bank." Johnny started shaking.

John pulled over and hugged his son, rubbing his shoulders. "It's alright Johnny, it happened a long time ago and it wasn't your fault." John reached in the back seat for a blanket, and wrapped it around Johnny. "Hang on son; I'm going to get you home as quick as I can."

John pulled into the driveway and Angie ran out and together they helped Johnny up to his room. Angie covered him with quilts and sat next to him hugging him, but his tears kept flowing.

"I'll see if I can get Doctor Evans' private number," John said.

John met Helen and Jenny in the hallway and explained the situation.

"Let's grab Grandpa and go have a little breakfast while we get a hold of this doctor," he suggested. "I think Angie's got a grip on things up here."

Doctor Evans called some prescriptions into the local pharmacy, and while Dad went to pick them up, Jenny and Grandpa went to bring the van home.

It was a quiet day in the Hendricks home. Late in the evening Johnny woke up and wanted to see Jenny.

"How'er ya feelin sweetie," she asked, sitting on the edge of the bed.

"Pretty rough," he said, in a raspy voice from all the weeping.

"We've all been praying for you all day. I wish there was some way we could take away your pain," Jenny said.

"I just can't understand why this thing hit me now."

"Just relax and go back to sleep. You've got the dream team watching over you. You've got God, and your Mom and Dad. You've got me and Helen and Grandpa, and if that's not enough, you probably got the whole Hackala family praying for you too. So get some rest big guy," she said as she leaned over and kissed him good night.

As she walked back down the stairs she wished that she was more confident than she felt.

$$\underline{\qquad\text{\Large ☀}\qquad}$$

CHAPTER 23

Sunday morning was controlled pandemonium as everyone but Johnny busily prepared themselves for church services. Grandpa was up and dressed early and sitting in the living room going over his sermon. John was on the telephone with one of his elders while Angie was dressed and in the kitchen cutting up a coffee cake. Helen and Jenny were still upstairs hoping they had brought the right outfits for their first Protestant worship service.

"I hope these clothes aren't too dressy," Helen said to Jenny while looking in the full length mirror.

"I suppose the worst that could happen is that they'll spot us for Catholics and drag us outside to the dunking stool," joked Jenny.

"Oh, I do wish Johnny was going with us," fretted Helen, he's been such a comfort on Sunday mornings."

"Those knock-out pills the doctor prescribed should have him dreaming until we all get back." Jenny said.

Jenny and Helen rode with John and Angie to the downtown Community Church, and were glad that they had because the Pastor's parking spot was right next to the building. Helen and Jenny felt like celebrities as they were greeted by dozens of people of every age, color and country of origin. Helen soon forgot her dress worries as people of every social stratum blended together as one Christian family.

"Where would you like to sit?" asked Angie as an usher escorted them down one of the side aisles.

"Anywhere is fine, Angie," Helen said to her hostess, "We're not particular."

By 10:00 a.m. the sanctuary was packed as John Hendricks approached the pulpit and smiled at his flock.

"Good morning my brothers and sisters in Christ," he said with a booming voice. "Although every time we meet together in the presence of God is very special, this morning Angie and I had hoped today would be extra special, because our son Johnny is home."

Everyone applauded and cheered.

"Unfortunately, as the old saying goes, you prepare for the best and then life gets in the way. I'm afraid that is what has happened this morning. Johnny got hit by some kind of a bug on Friday night that hospitalized him and now he is home in bed wishing he was here. You know he would love to see and greet all of you, but that will have to wait a little while. He hopes you understand."

Everyone murmured and shook their heads in agreement.

"But, he did bring down two friends with him from Hancock who are both instrumental in getting the new mission started. I would like to introduce them to you right now. Ladies, can I get you to stand for a moment so that our congregation can honor you?" John asked.

Helen and Jenny looked at each other and both of them slowly stood. A thunderous round of applause embarrassed both of them as they demurely sat down. John went on with the service. The choir sang, scripture was read and John gave an inspirational message about the world being one community and we are all God's children. After the service John of course had to shake hands with everybody, so, the three ladies went down to the fellowship hall and ate cookies, drank punch and acted like celebrities. John had an emergency finance meeting after the fellowship hour, so it was well after noon before they were in the car and headed home.

"I'm sure Grandpa's home already," said Angie, so let's pick up some chicken, and we'll have a picnic in the den."

"Without the ants," added Dad.

An hour later, everybody had changed to more comfortable clothing and sat lounging in the den. Johnny came down the stairs in his bathrobe and flopped down on the sofa.

"Well good afternoon sunshine, how are you feeling?" Angie asked.

"A little groggy and definitely hungry," Johnny responded. "Is that fried chicken I smell?"

"Yes," Jenny said. "Can I fix you a plate?"

"Please," he said, "with double mashed potatoes and gravy. So, how was church?" he asked his Dad. "Did you delicately explain my absence?"

"The whole church felt badly that you were under the weather, but I explained that it was only temporary and that you would be back on your feet in no time."

"I wish I was as sure of that as you are," Johnny said, accepting a plate of food from Jenny.

"Well, how are you feeling right now, Johnny?" asked Grandpa.

"Actually, I feel great, but I've got to confess I'm a little frightened. It's kind of like carrying a time bomb in your brain and you don't know when or why it's going to go off."

"Johnny," Helen said, sitting next to Grandpa on the couch, "If it wouldn't be too painful, could you tell me exactly what happened. I guess everyone here knows, but me."

It was difficult for Johnny to remember how he felt or what he remembered, but in a short while he realized that he didn't want to remember. It was so long ago that it wasn't relevant in his life any more.

"Helen, I really don't know what to say or how I'm feeling," he said apologetically.

"Well let me say something then," she said gaining confidence. "I came down here four days ago expecting the vacation of a life time. I've never been much nor done anything special in my life and always pretty much kept to myself, but you," she said looking at Johnny, "you came into my life like a whirlwind and changed all that. I was perfectly happy to end my days trudging through life minding my own business, but not anymore." Helen stopped and looked around the room. "Now, all five of you sitting here are more intelligent and better educated than I am, but I'll tell you what I've learned in the last two days and maybe it will make sense."

The other five people in the room slid back in their seats and set down their dinners as the *Oracle* from Hancock, in the form of Helen, began her supposition.

"First of all, the Bible teaches us that everyone is born to die and everyone in this room has lost some one who we have loved deeply. But," she said making a point, "the difference between losing one's life naturally or unexpectedly and how we deal with it is what we are confronting today. Johnny, I'm going to tell you two stories."

Helen told Johnny how she had told his family about the death of her son, Stevie, on their ride home from the hospital. A story she had told no one about since his death. "I don't know why it just sort of jumped out of my mouth, but I have a feeling that it had been hiding in my heart for a long time and needed to be released to make room for more love."

Helen was still for a moment and then looked at Angie. "And not three hours later," she added, "your mother told me about losing her younger brother, your Uncle Jose, who disappeared mysteriously while traveling in Mexico, and was never seen again. What I'm trying to say Johnny, is that that loss of someone special is so traumatically sad that we try to keep it buried from ourselves to avoid the inner grief. That doesn't make us monsters, Johnny. That only makes us human. We give that grief to God and pray that our loved ones are with Him and at peace and away from all of this unhappiness. Am I making any sense at all?'

"Can I hear an Amen," shouted Grandpa. "I think we've got us another preacher."

"What a wonderful thought," echoed Angie. "God has truly blessed us by bringing you two ladies into our home this weekend."

Johnny walked over and kissed Helen on the cheek. "You know," he said to the others, "she doesn't have a college degree, but she eats Thimbleberries every day, and that ought to count for something."

The afternoon ran its course with small talk and laughter. Helen asked Johnny to bring down the surprise package that he had complained about while they were packing the van. With great exertion, Johnny dragged the heavy bag down the stairs and set it on the table.

"Now I know what you're thinking," Helen said. "This is probably some old tea set that my Aunt Tilly handed down to me that I'm trying to pawn off on you, but you're wrong."

Everyone in the room was in such great spirits now that they all feigned disappointment at the loss of one of Tilly's heirlooms.

"No," she said, "this is slightly more valuable and infinitely more precious because of its importance to your family, your churches and the Mission Johnny Hendricks will soon be founding on Quincy Street in Hancock, Michigan."

Helen held everyone's attention as she stood up and folded back the large plastic bag. What lay inside was a filthy burlap bag containing something slightly larger than a bowling ball.

"Now I'm going to tell you a story," she said. "When my husband Arvin's father signed the papers to buy the Aho Building, the previous owner told him to sit right where he was. The man disappeared down the basement stairs and came back up with this same dirty bag and set it on the floor in front of Arvin's dad. The story goes that when the original basement was dug on Quincy Street, this large boulder of pure copper came rolling out of the hole and the land owner claimed it as a souvenir. Now, mining had changed by the time Hancock city was built and extracting pure copper was a thing of the past. So, this huge nugget was a real find, kind of like finding a large uncut diamond. Well, the story goes, that every time the building was sold, this 'paperweight' as they called it, was part of the deal. It was kind of a rich man's memento, I suppose."

As she opened the sack, Johnny said, "What are we suppose to do with it?"

Everyone crowded around and touched its jagged edges.

"I don't know," Helen said, "but somehow God chose you to resurrect the old building so maybe it might become a symbol of a new era or something. At any rate, I want your family to have it to do with as you will," she said.

The afternoon quickly passed and Johnny said he felt well enough to travel the next day. The packing began and all too soon the van was gassed up and loaded for the journey home on Monday.

CHAPTER 24

Long before sunrise John, Angie and Dutch stood in their pajamas in the kitchen and hugged the travelers one more time.

"If I might be permitted," Dad said, wrapping his arms around the other five.

> *"Almighty God, you have filled our home with joy and love this weekend and for that we are all grateful, but you have also taught us that You are always there to help us find our way when we seem the most lost. Please grant travel mercies to these three fine children of yours that they might go forward and do your work. Amen."*

"Thank you, John," said Helen. "You don't know how much that means to me."

"Well, you better be on your way if you're going to have pasties for dinner," Grandpa joked.

The three travelers climbed into the van while Dad scraped the windshield. Two minutes later they were on the

Interstate 96 loop around Grand Rapids headed for U.S. 131 north and home.

By the time they reached Rockford, Johnny could hear Helen snoring softly in the back seat. He and Jenny smiled at each other like a couple of parents who finally got the kids to go to sleep. Monday morning traffic was heavy, but they felt like they were in their own little world as a couple for the first time.

"Did you have a good time?" he asked, taking Jenny's hand.

"I don't think I've ever been happier," she said.

Johnny squeezed her hand, "That makes two of us." They rode along without speaking for a little while. "You know, yesterday morning," Johnny said, "while you were in church, I made a couple of phone calls."

"Who'd you call?" Jenny asked.

"First I called Ernie to see how R.J. was doing."

"And?"

"Judge Tumi is having a hearing tomorrow morning, and according to Ernie, R.J. has made amends to all of the people that he stole from and it looks like he'll be moving in with Ernie and Brenda in a couple of weeks."

"Wow that was fast!" Jenny said.

"Yeah they're all pretty excited about it."

"And what was the other call?' asked Jenny getting more excited.

"This one was even better." Johnny said.

"What!" she shouted waking up Helen.

"What's going on up there?" Helen asked

"Nothing," said Johnny, "Go back to sleep."

Helen reached for a blanket, placed it up against the window, and dozed off again.

"Anyway," Johnny teased, "I called Howard to see how his holiday was…"

"And" Jenny said nearly exasperated.

"He and Maggie have invited Kitty and Jimmy to come and live with them. They have two extra bed rooms, and Maggie can take Jimmy up to physical therapy everyday while Kitty sleeps. Howard even mentioned something about having Kitty take some secretarial courses at Finlandia University and maybe help him around the office. He said Jimmy's mother shouldn't be working in a bar.

"You're kidding," Jenny shouted again, "That's wonderful."

"What's wonderful," asked Helen finally sitting up and straightening her hair.

"Helen, everything God touches is wonderful if you just give it enough time," Johnny said winking at Jenny.

It was hard to believe that he had only left home a month and a half ago full of hopes and anxieties with all kinds of preconceived notions of what his future would bring. And now here he was driving the same road with new direction and purpose. Johnny looked over at Jenny who had dozed off with the hood of her parka cushioning her head against the frosty window. He was so grateful that God had brought these two wonderful women into his life, and how different his life would be if he hadn't checked the bulletin board at Kaleva's that first morning in Hancock and spotted Helen's card.

The traffic eased up, the weather brightened and Johnny began to plan his agenda as he drove passed the Cadillac exit. First he would call a meeting of the new Hancock Youth Council and Mission Project and officially install Howard Berg as the first President of the organization. Then collectively evaluate what they had and where they were, and most importantly where they wanted to go with this program. Johnny had a lot of ideas, and he imagined the rest of the members did too. The next order of business was to write an editorial in the Mining Gazette explaining the co-operative effort between the city council, the HHCA and community itself in forming a new Hancock Youth Mission in the Aho Building, for the benefit of all of the teens in the area. Johnny was so excited he could hardly keep the van on the road.

As he approached M-32 to cut over to I-75, Jenny stretched and asked Johnny?" What are you grinning about?"

"What's the biggest place in Hancock to hold a community Christmas party?" He asked.

"I don't know. What do you have in mind?" she asked.

'Peace on earth," he said. "Peace on earth."

ABOUT THE AUTHOR

Holmes draws on the experiences of his own youth in creating this story of Johnny Hendricks, whose faith and calling bring him to the tip of Michigan's Upper Peninsula.

Over the last forty years, Brian and his family have made excursions to the Keweenaw Peninsula and have tried to absorb this culture woven between Finnish American tradition and a failed copper-mining economy. Hopefully, this tale will present the challenges Johnny faces at every turn, and through hard work, and the hand of God, wins the day.